Queen Hustlaz
Part 2

Queen Hustlaz
Part 2

Falicia Love

www.urbanbooks.net

Urban Books, LLC
300 Farmingdale Road, NY-Route 109
Farmingdale, NY 11735

Queen Hustlaz Part 2 © 2018 Falicia Love

ISBN 13: 978-1-62286-187-3
ISBN 10: 1-62286-187-6

First Mass Market Printing October 2019
First Trade Paperback Printing May 2018
Printed in the United States of America

10 9 8 7 6 5 4 3 2 1

This is a work of fiction. Any references or similarities to actual events, real people, living or dead, or to real locales are intended to give the novel a sense of reality. Any similarity in other names, characters, places, and incidents is entirely coincidental.

Distributed by Kensington Publishing Corp.
Submit Orders to:
Customer Service
400 Hahn Road
Westminster, MD 21157-4627
Phone: 1-800-733-3000
Fax: 1-800-659-2436

Dedication

I dedicate this novel first to my lovely daughter, Miss Candise Love! You are all the inspiration a mother needs to keep going. I love you, baby!

To my fam facing time behind the fence, y'all know I love you all and I pray every day that you guys find some sort of peace with y'all situation: Travis Love, Derek Love, Willie Moore, Tino Love, Toby Love, and Uncle Ronnie Love.

To my family and friends who have passed away: Benny Love Jr., my son, li'l Nate Herbin Jr., Nathaniel D. Herbin, Mortrice Marley, Elijah Carroway, and "Rick Rick Moore." You will never be forgotten!

Acknowledgments

First and foremost, thank God for allowing me to complete my first Urban series.

Thanks to my family: Shirley Love, Valerie Love, Barney Jr. Love, Selina Miles, my wonderful nieces, nephews, and cousins for standing behind me on this project. I love each of you for being who you are.

Meldamion Huguley aka Damion King: thanks for being supportive. We still grinding, dude. Love you!

Ebony Rone and Jasper Thaxton: You both are a part of the family, and I got to shout you two out.

Okay, now for the readers: Tina Baker (cuzzz), Sherry Boose, Denise Relerford, La'Shan Michele, Kendra Huskey, Viola King, Jane Penella, Joan Brooks, Carol King, A'karies My World, Katanya Williams, Redgirl Pettrie, Pamela Ward, Joan Brooks and Carol Mustipher, and everyone else who has supported me.

Acknowledgments

To My RWP fam: I thank each one of you for all the team support. We are fam no matter what.

Racquel Williams, you are the best! Thanks a lot for giving me this opportunity.

All right, y'all, I'm done. Hope you enjoy this finale!

Prologue

Jeryca Mebane was faced with a decision to make. She was ready to venture out on her own, feeling like Dana and Stephanie were holding her back. Orlando had shown her that he was going to be there for her and she needed that in her life. All the things that she had been learning and seeing from Dana, Stephanie, and Brittany lately she didn't want to be a part of any longer, and she was definitely going to find her way completely out. After seeing Brenda in the hospital, she knew that Dana's time was coming near.

Dana was fighting to make sense out of everything. She had mixed feelings about the fact that she had killed Farrah, and guilt was in her heart. But she knew she couldn't let the guilt get to her, as she had plans of taking everybody down. She felt that her friends weren't really down with her like they said they were, and she was going to have to watch them close. As the old saying goes, "Keep your friends close and your enemies closer." Frienemies were what she called them.

Recap

Friday morning, Dana went to work and walked into Brittany's office. "Have you talked to Orlando or Zack today?"

"Yeah, they called me about thirty minutes ago, checking in as usual. Why? What's up?" Brittany asked.

"Girl, I guess I'm just paranoid about the whole Debra situation," Dana answered.

"You still on that? I told you I would handle the situation, but we don't need any unnecessary attention drawn to us. We are running a law firm that is well-established, and I don't need any unwanted or unnecessary scrutiny from the law. You know just like I do that a lot of things I do aren't one hundred percent legit, so feel how you want to feel, but I'm not going to move recklessly because you want me to!" Brittany snapped.

"You know what, Brittany? I never thought you would show a shady side. Now where was all that talk when things got out of control with Farrah? You were praising me for that, but when it's your turn to fix shit, you find every excuse why you can't! Tell me, why is that?" Dana asked angrily.

"I don't have to explain shit. I just said what I had to say, Dana, and if you can't comprehend the truth that isn't my fault. Just like it isn't my fault that you been running around town half damn cocked. Yeah, I praised you for doing what you been doing, but, girl, you can't keep trying to do things to jeopardize what we got going on," Brittany said, getting agitated.

"Whatever, Brittany! I think I am going to leave early today. I'm suddenly feeling sick," Dana replied.

Brittany looked at Dana long and hard, and without batting an eye, she said, "Suck it up. There's work that needs to be done. Get out your fucking feelings and complete those files that are on your desk. Our clients don't pay us big money to get sick out of the blue and put they shit to the side. If that's a problem, Dana, I can find someone else to do your work for you permanently. It's nothing personal, but I have a business to run, little girl."

Dana felt like she wanted to cry. Brittany had never spoken to her in that tone, and she was deeply affected by that. Dana shook her head. "I got it."

"Good. Now, please trust me a little bit, Dana. I know what I'm doing," Brittany said.

Dana walked out of Brittany's office and didn't say a word. Brittany stared at the door for a few seconds after Dana left.

"Baby girl might become a problem," she muttered to herself. Brittany picked up the phone and called the one person she assumed could talk to Dana.

Dana sat down at her desk, angry and hurt. She felt that betrayal was all around her. She needed to get away and quick. She needed the money from the robbery they pulled on Thad, and then she was going to bounce. She had decided to tell Zack and Brittany that she was out of the next robbery. She felt that she couldn't trust them and she wasn't going to set herself up for failure.

She sighed and pulled a file from her drawer to begin doing an analysis of the case. After fifteen minutes, her phone rang. "Holmes, Howell and Fuller Associates."

"Hey, it's Zack. What's up, Dana?" he asked.

"Hey, Zack, how are you doing?" Dana asked, frowning. She didn't know why he was calling her on the office phone rather than on her cell.

"Shit, nothing. I just talked to Britt and was wondering if we could meet somewhere later and talk," he replied.

Dana laughed and shook her head. "Wow, you too. This is too much for me."

"Hold up. It ain't no 'you too.' First of all, I just wanted to check to make sure you are good. So you can kill the attitude!" Zack retorted.

"You know what? First of all," Dana mimicked, "you have never called my office phone, so that makes you suspect in my book, and second of all, don't ever speak to me in that damn tone. Y'all got shit twisted!"

Zack laughed. "I'm not even going to respond, Dana. Can we meet or not?" he asked again.

"Maybe tomorrow. I'm busy tonight," Dana answered. She wasn't busy, but she wasn't going to meet him anywhere. She had to gather her thoughts and find a way for her to win without any of them.

"All right, Dana. Look, I don't know what's going on with you, but please chill out with the extra drama," Zack said.

"I hear you. I got to go," Dana said and hung up. Dana was heated. She wanted to cuss Brittany out for calling Zack, but she refrained from doing it.

She worked on her case file until noon and decided to call Stephanie up. She needed a night out. She hadn't talked to her since they had words about Stephanie and Jeryca fighting. They talked for an hour and decided that they would meet at the Oasis to get a few drinks.

Stephanie asked Robin to join them, and she happily agreed. Stephanie and Robin decided to go out to dinner before they met Dana at the club. They discussed things they each wanted to do before they died.

"Bae, I want to go to Hawaii. I want to put on a grass skirt and dance barefoot in the sand," Robin said, staring off into space.

Stephanie could see by the look in her eyes when she talked about it how important it was to Robin to go to Hawaii. "I'm going to make it happen for you, Robin. If I don't do anything else, I'm taking you to Hawaii," Stephanie said.

Robin smiled at Stephanie and took a sip of her wine. "Babe, I believe you. Are you ready to go to the Oasis?"

"You don't believe me, but I'm serious. We are going to go and soon," Stephanie said as she stood up and laid a tip on the table.

Robin knew that Stephanie was serious, but she didn't want her to feel as if she had to do it.

After they paid the bill, they left and headed to the Oasis. When they got there, Dana hadn't arrived, so they grabbed a table and ordered a few drinks. Stephanie was enjoying herself until her eyes landed on Chris.

"Shit, what the hell is he doing here?" she half whispered to herself. He was smiling at her and Robin didn't miss the look exchanged between the two.

"Bae, who is that?" Robin asked, already knowing the answer.

Stephanie looked at her and muttered, "That's Chris."

"Well, I will say you got great taste in women as well as men." Robin laughed as she leaned over and kissed Stephanie.

A few minutes later Chris was making his way to Stephanie's table. "How are you doing, Stephanie?" he asked.

I'm good, Chris. How are you?" she replied.

"I'm good. You still looking good, Stephanie," he said, smiling.

"This is my baby, Robin. Robin, this is my ex, Chris," Stephanie replied, ignoring Chris's last comment.

"How are you? Damn, you are a sexy li'l thang also. I'd love to buy you two ladies a drink," Chris drawled.

"Thank you, and yes, you can buy us a drink," Robin answered before Stephanie could refuse.

"All right, what do you want?" Chris asked.

"I want a Tom Collins," Robin said, smiling.

"I don't want anything, thanks," Stephanie replied.

"Come on, Steph, don't be like that. I'm just trying to be a nice guy," Chris said.

"I'm good, Chris. I got a drink right here," Stephanie replied.

"All right, maybe later," he said as he walked to the bar to get Robin's drink.

Stephanie looked at Robin and grabbed her hand roughly. "Bae, you can't play with a man like Chris. I see it in your face, all the flirting and shit. Don't do that."

"It's harmless, Steph," Robin laughed, using the nickname Chris used for her.

"To you it's harmless, but to him, it's something else. Please just listen to me on this," Stephanie said.

When Chris returned, Thad and Toby accompanied him. "Hey, lady, long time no see," Thad said.

"Yeah, it's been a while. How is the family?" Stephanie asked. She wasn't feeling the whole situation at all. She didn't want to see them at all. She knew that they were after the people who robbed them, and she didn't want to set off the wrong vibe.

"Everyone is good. Sorry to hear about Farrah. We been meaning to go by Shirley's house to check on Travis, but for some reason, we just haven't made it," Toby said, smiling at Robin.

Stephanie noticed the look and immediately introduced her. "This is my girlfriend, Robin. Robin, this is Thad and Toby."

Everyone talked for a few minutes longer, but then they were interrupted by Dana. "Well, ain't this cozy."

"Hey, come on and have a seat," Stephanie said quickly.

Dana sat down and looked at Thad long and hard, without cracking one smile. She didn't speak to any of the guys at the table, period.

Chris excused himself, along with Thad and Toby, but not before Thad broke the silence between him and Dana. "Dana, you're looking gorgeous as ever. By the way, have you heard from Keith lately? He seems to have disappeared with some things that belong to me."

"I haven't heard from Keith in a while. Enjoy your night, fellows," Dana replied, before turning her attention to Robin. "How are you doing, Ms. Robin?"

Once the men were gone, Dana looked at Stephanie. "What the fuck did they want?"

"Shit, Chris came over first, and before we knew it, we were surrounded by their asses," Stephanie answered.

"Well, anyway, I'ma go get me a drink. I'll be right back, okay?" Dana replied. She stood up and walked to the bar.

When she returned, she sat down, and the ladies talked about several things. They were enjoying the atmosphere in the Oasis. They had drunk several drinks, so one girl after the other had to take a bathroom break. When Robin stood up for the third time and excused herself from the table to go to the restroom, Chris, who had been checking the ladies' table out all night, followed her to the bathroom door. He blocked her entrance and smiled. "Stephanie got her a fine-ass chick."

"She sure does, and I got me a fine-ass female as well, and I plan on keeping her," Robin stated flatly.

"Listen, I'm not trying to stop what y'all got going on, but I need to talk with Steph, one-on-one. Do you think that will be possible?" he asked.

Robin laughed. "When pigs fly!" she answered.

"Shit, I can make that happen, baby girl," he replied.

"Listen, I got to go in here and piss, and get back to my baby. So unless there is anything else you want, move," Robin demanded.

"All right, all right. Don't get so defensive. Look, here is my number. Call me and let's chat about it," Chris said as he wrote his number down on a napkin and placed it in her pocket.

Robin rolled her eyes and pushed past him into the restroom. After she finished, she stood looking in the mirror and then at the number Chris handed her. She didn't know why she wasn't throwing it away, because she knew deep down that she was playing with fire.

She returned to the table, and the ladies danced and enjoyed the rest of their night, without any further interruptions from Chris or his crew.

Saturday morning, Stephanie lay in bed, thinking about Chris. She couldn't believe that he cornered her in the bathroom at the Oasis last night, and attempted to fondle her and kiss her. She'd fought him off and walked quickly back to the table where Dana and Robin were waiting. She didn't tell Robin what had happened, but she wanted to. The kiss that Chris had planted on her left her lips—both sets—tingling. She loved Robin, but she ached for Chris.

She shook her head as if she were trying to shake the thought of Chris from her head.

"Hey, bae, I'm 'bout to head on to work, okay? I love you," Robin said as she leaned down to give Stephanie a kiss.

Stephanie grabbed Robin's face to prolong the kiss. "You got to go now? I know you got a few minutes to spare."

"Bae, I got twenty minutes to get to work so, no, I don't have spare time. I'll see you tonight." Robin laughed as she walked out the door.

"Oh, well. I got to do something. I'm horny," she said quietly. She searched the drawer, pulled out her vibrator, put lubrication on it, and lay back. She climaxed twice with Chris on her mind.

Robin arrived at work and started counting out medication. She was amazed at how Chris and Dana were acting last night. At first, she had an issue with him calling her, but for some reason, she found herself sexually attracted to him. Although she wasn't going to give Stephanie up to him, she was definitely game for sharing her with him. She wanted a threesome, and if he could fuck as good as he looked, it could be a regular occurrence. She figured she would run that idea by Stephanie when she clocked out for lunch.

The morning seemed to creep by, and she couldn't wait to call Stephanie. Once she clocked out, she called Stephanie and got no answer. She tried a second time and still got no answer. She pulled the number out from her wallet and dialed Chris up.

"Yeah, who is this?" he asked.

"This is Robin. You haven't by any chance seen Stephanie?" she asked, holding her breath, hoping he would say no.

"Maybe I have, maybe I haven't. You can come see for yourself if you like," he moaned.

"Where are you at?" she asked. Robin knew that Stephanie wasn't there, but for some reason, she had to go see to be sure.

Chris gave her the hotel's address and room number, and they ended the call. For the rest of the afternoon, Robin worked hard to push away the thought of her, Chris, and Stephanie getting together.

When five o'clock came, she rushed out to her car and dialed Stephanie's number.

"Hello," Stephanie answered.

"I have been calling you all day, boo. What's going on? Where you been?" Robin asked.

"I went to see my cousin, and we kicked it for a while. I called you back, but I guess you were back on the clock. What do you want me to cook for dinner?" Stephanie asked.

"Oh um, bae, I'm going to be a little late tonight. We got to do med pull and got a new shipment coming in," Robin lied.

"All right. I got to deal with it, I guess," Stephanie said sadly.

"You know I'ma make it up to you," Robin stated.

"I know you will. I love you," Stephanie said.

"I love you too. I'm going to call you back later, okay?" Robin replied.

After she hung up, she drove to the Ramada Inn and Suites and went to the room that Chris told her he was in. She knocked three times, and finally, Chris opened the door.

He looked shocked at first then he smiled. "I didn't think you were coming."

"Well, I just wanted to make sure my girl not here," she replied.

"Come on in and see for yourself," Chris said, as he moved to allow her to enter.

As he closed the door, he smiled. He knew that she knew Stephanie wasn't there. It was kind of bittersweet.

"So take a look around and see if your girl-friend is here." Chris laughed.

Robin turned around, looked Chris in the eyes, and said provocatively, "You and I both know that I know Stephanie isn't here, so let's stop playing. You see, I refuse to lose my bae to you, but after seeing the chemistry you two have, I know there's something there. I think we can all form some sort of relationship, so I'm here to see what you're working with."

"Is that right? Well, we can definitely do that," Chris replied, as he walked toward Robin. He grabbed her by her waist and walked her backward toward the bed. When he laid her on the bed, he undressed her and then himself, and he smiled once he saw the look on her face. She looked frightened, which made him laugh aloud. "This is going to be fun."

An hour later, Robin walked out of his hotel room, fully satisfied and content. She understood now why Stephanie was fucked up about him. Once she arrived home and walked into her apartment, Stephanie was sitting on the couch, waiting for her.

"Did you work hard, bae?" she asked.

"Yes. I'm tired, so I'm going to take a shower, and we can eat dinner, okay?" Robin said walking toward the bathroom.

"I didn't cook dinner yet, but let me ask you a question before you get in the shower," Stephanie said.

"Go 'head, bae," Robin said, kicking her shoes off.

"If you were at work, why when I called down there did they say you were already gone for the day?" Stephanie asked.

Robin looked at her for a moment, then replied, "We did inventory at the main pharmacy, Stephanie. Why are you questioning me about being at work, when you know that's all I do?"

"Bae, I was just heated 'cause they told me you weren't there and you told me you were working overtime. I'm not accusing you of anything," Stephanie explained.

"You know you got me, girl, and I'm not going anywhere," Robin said, looking Stephanie in the face.

Stephanie could see that Robin was sincere about what she was saying, and she smiled. "I know, bae."

Robin prepared her water and got into the shower. As she washed her still-pulsating clit, she couldn't help but smile. She had done a very bad thing, but it felt so damn good.

Chapter One

Monday morning around four-thirty, Austin pulled up in front of Thad's trap house in a blue Chevy van that he had been working on for a client. The client never picked it up, so he figured that, by using this van, it wouldn't be traceable to any of them. He had Leon and Vince in a white car trailing behind him. They weren't going to take part in the robbery at all. Their only job was to wait outside until after the robbery, and then they would help load the boxes into the van and take it to a storage unit that Thad had rented a few weeks earlier.

They had been planning for this moment. He blew the horn twice, and five minutes later, Thad came out.

"What's up, playa?" Austin said once Thad was seated in the van.

"I'm just ready to get this money, Austin. We got to go get Toby and Chris. Then we can go on and hit Orlando's shit! I have a source who has assured me that we will get more than we initially estimated," Thad replied.

"Word! That's all good with me!" Austin said.

"Ay, is Chris with you, bro? I hope y'all ready. We ain't got time to mess around," Thad said into his cell phone.

"Is that Toby?" Austin whispered.

Thad nodded and continued talking. "All right, we will be there in about ten minutes or so."

"Tell Toby to make sure he gets the coats and face masks," Austin mumbled.

"Oh yeah, bro, you got our gear, right? All right then, get it all together and be ready," Thad said, as he concluded his call.

Austin drove straight to Toby's house, and once Toby and Chris were in the van, they hit the highway with Orlando's warehouse as their destination.

Chris was sitting in the back, getting himself mentally prepared for the robbery. He still hadn't heard from Debra, and he was now getting worried. He hoped that no one had found out about her taking part of the lick that Larry pulled. He couldn't live with himself if something happened to her. He had talked her into helping Larry after she came to him with her doubts about doing it. He had a gut feeling though that something just wasn't right. If anyone had harmed her, he would see that they paid dearly.

"Chris, take this gun and mask. Let's make sure we straight by the time we get there. We should be there in about thirty minutes. I hope Orlando is there so I can pop his ass. I need that nigga out the way for real," Thad said.

Chris took the gun and mask and placed them on his lap. Toby was nodding off next to him, which had him wondering how he could be sleeping at a time like that.

Chris wasn't happy being in the van with Thad and Toby. He really had lost all respect for them, but he needed to make some loot off the robbery so he could work his way up and out of the game. He just hoped Debra was still alive to enjoy a new lifestyle with him.

"All right, we're here! I'ma pull around to the side. It looks like they are just getting here to open so, once we pull up, Thad, you know what you got to do. Jump out and grab that first nigga and put that pistol to his cranium," Toby said, as Austin switched the headlights off before creeping around the side of the building.

"Man, I know what I got to do. You just be in place to run up quick and grab the other two motherfuckers," Thad said.

Austin crept up and stopped a few feet short of where the three men were standing, preparing to unlock the door. He shut the motor off, and

Thad quietly got out of the car, with Chris and Toby behind him. Thad immediately ran up, threw the gun up toward the first man's head, and whispered, "Don't none of you bastards move or say one word, or I will blow this faggot's head off. Open the door now!"

By that time, Toby had his beam on the second guy, and Chris was on the third guy, pushing him into the warehouse after the door was unlocked.

"Turn the lights on!" Chris ordered one of the men.

Once the lights were on, they tied two of the men up but left Tim untied. Tim was Orlando's right-hand man. Thad knew who he was when they first rolled up on them. If anybody knew where the guns and drugs were, it was Tim.

"Before we start hearing the bullshit-ass lies, we know what you are going to try to tell us. We know for a fact that there are guns and cocaine located in this warehouse. Show us where they are and we can get out of here, and no one will get hurt," Toby snarled.

"I don't know what you're talking about. Really, I don't," Tim cried.

Toby turned his head slightly toward Thad, who just shook his head. He turned back to face Tim and hit him across the face with the gun, knocking him to the floor.

Tim got back up and yelled, with blood trickling down the side of his head, "Man, do you know who the fuck I am? You are making a grave mistake!"

"Motherfucker, shut the fuck up! Who the hell cares who you are? Show us where the damn shit is at so we can be on our way," Toby growled, ready to explode.

Tim staggered toward the west wing of the warehouse with Toby and Austin in tow. Chris and Thad stayed with the other two guys, making sure no one either came in or left. After a few moments passed, Toby yelled for Thad to get Leon and Vince in there, so they could get the crates and load them up.

Once everything was loaded, Toby stood in front of all three men and smiled. "You know, I told you that if no one lied to us and gave us what we wanted, I wouldn't kill anyone. But, nigga, you lied straight from the gate, and for that, you got to die! I mean, I am a man of my word."

Toby raised his gun, and before any word was uttered, he shot Tim in the face. Tim dropped to the floor, and Toby stood over him, shooting him five more times.

He looked at Thad and Chris and walked out. Thad shot the other two guys in the back of the head, and he and Chris ran out and jumped into the van. They drove to the storage unit and piled the crates inside.

Afterward, the men went to Austin's cousin's chop shop and dropped the car and van off, so that his cousin could flip the vehicles and sell them. They were hyped up and weren't ready to turn down. They went to their favorite strip club, the Oasis.

They sat down in front, and the strippers immediately flocked to their table. They knew they had some big spenders in their establishment. There weren't many patrons around, and Toby figured it was probably because it was only noon.

Thad nudged Toby and smiled. "Bro, I am so proud of you. We did that shit, my nigga."

"Boy, it felt good squeezing on that bitch nigga! I swear I feel rejuvenated. We back in there, too. Did you see all that shit we loaded up? Two more hits like that and we will be able to pay Sergio and Ramon back what we owe them, and still be able to make our own play with them and bring in our connects from North Carolina," Toby replied excitedly.

"I know, but who should we hit up next? Rob may be a possible candidate. You know he got that dope and loot," Thad commented as one of the strippers was shaking her ass in front of his face. Thad reached up, swatted her butt a few times, and placed a twenty-dollar bill in her G-string. Then she dropped down on his lap and started grinding on him.

"Ay, boy, I like the sound of hitting Rob's ass," Austin agreed. "He won't even know what hit him. We can run in and out of his spot real quick. Shit, we trying to live and eat so anybody can get it. Nobody is safe from us."

"I'm with that!" Toby said as he watched his brother suck on the stripper's nipples. Toby shook his head and laughed. "Nigga, you don't know whose mouth been on her tits! You gotta use some kind of restraint."

Thad looked up at the stripper. "I know I need to use restraint, but damn she fine as hell!"

Austin laughed. "You might as well be kissing all these niggas in here, dude, 'cause you know how some of these niggas are. They suck 'em and fuck 'em!"

"Y'all sure do know how to spoil a nigga's good time!" Thad said, and he stood up and walked to the restroom to wash his mouth out.

Orlando and Jeryca awoke at ten-thirty Monday morning, and he rushed to get dressed. He was running late and had to check in at the warehouse before he took Jeryca home.

As they rolled down highway 115-N, Brooklyn, Jeryca couldn't get over the happiness she was feeling. She had never lain in a man's arms all night and just cuddled. She always had to put out. She actually enjoyed being treated like the lady she always knew she was. She was going to introduce Orlando to her sister, Pam, that evening. Orlando was more than ready to meet her. He was planning to take her mother and Pam out to dinner that evening. She couldn't wait for them to see what a prize he was.

Once they pulled up to the building, Orlando quickly noticed how dark it was in the warehouse. None of the lights were on. The building was shut up, and there was no type of activity.

"Bae, stay in the car. I'll be right back," Orlando told Jeryca.

"Orlando, I don't want to stay in the car. If you are going in, I'm going in with you," she said, getting out of the car.

"Girl, get your butt back in there. I won't be but a hot minute," Orlando replied.

"We won't be but a hot minute," Jeryca stated, determined that she wasn't going to be left out in the car.

Orlando shook his head and grabbed Jeryca by the hand. "Come on here, girl!"

Jeryca smiled and followed Orlando into the building.

As soon as he unlocked the door, he pulled his Glock from its holster. "Don't say shit!" he whispered to Jeryca.

She nodded, but she was growing more and more terrified by the minute. For a second, she wished she had stayed in the car. There was an eerie silence in the warehouse, and Orlando knew something was wrong.

As they slowly walked farther into the warehouse, Orlando finally spotted what he feared he would. Tim's body was sprawled out on the floor in a pool of blood. Orlando blinked several times and squatted next to Tim's body. "Who the fuck . . ."

His words trailed off as he looked up and caught sight of Patrick's and Isaac's bodies. He stood up, and as Jeryca's gaze followed his, she let out a deafening scream. Orlando grabbed her. "Jeryca, be quiet! I know this isn't easy to see, but we don't want to draw any attention to us. Dammit!" Orlando immediately pulled out his cell phone and called Sergio and Ramon. He knew that where he found one, he would find both of them.

"Sergio, this is Orlando. We have a major problem that I know you would want to know about. I just walked into my warehouse and Tim is dead, Sergio. I don't know what happened, but he and two of my other men are dead."

There was a moment of silence on Orlando's end, but Jeryca heard a bunch of talking on the other end. She couldn't quite make out what was being said, but she could tell that whomever Orlando was talking to was very upset. Finally, Orlando cleared his throat and spoke. "All right, I got you. I'm 'bout to do that now. All right, the only thing I can think of that's here is the surveillance tape," Orlando said, and then there was another brief moment of silence. "I'ma get that and get my lady to take it to the car; then I will call the police. Damn, man, I just can't believe this shit! Not Tim!" Orlando cried.

After another pause, Orlando dropped his head. "I'm okay. I just can't believe this. I will call y'all later and set y'all up in a suite when you get here."

After Orlando hung up, he walked into his office, removed a video cassette from the recording machine, and handed Jeryca three tapes. "Take these to the car and wait for me outside while I contact the police."

Jeryca did as Orlando asked her to do. She could relate to how Orlando was feeling because she was still dealing with losing her friend.

It didn't take the police long to get to the warehouse once Orlando called them. The coroner's office came after the crime scene unit finished up.

Jeryca stood next to Orlando through everything. She really cared about him and hated seeing him as he was.

Orlando and Jeryca were taken down to police headquarters and interviewed by Detective Haith. She was a large woman and seemed angry out of the gate. The way she was talking to Jeryca had her feeling as if she was being accused of something. Jeryca continued to deny being there when everything happened or knowing anything about the killings. After a few hours of being interrogated, the detective had no other choice but to release Orlando and Jeryca. She didn't have any evidence or just cause to hold them. She warned them not to leave town and that they might need to talk with them again.

As the two left the police station, Jeryca watched Orlando very closely. He looked beat and worn. He opened her car door, got into the driver's side, and pulled off without saying a word.

He passed the exit to Jeryca's house and prayed she didn't ask him to take her home. He didn't want to be alone, period. When he felt her hand slide on top of his, he sighed, and for the first time ever, Jeryca witnessed a grown man cry. Silent tears slipped down his face, and he was biting his bottom lip.

She reached over and wiped the tears from his face. "It's okay, baby. I'm going to be here for you. You know I got you."

Orlando smiled because he knew she was telling the truth. He had to call Sergio once he got home and tell him what had occurred at the police station, but first, he wanted to look at the video surveillance tapes.

They pulled up to Orlando's house, and he sat in the car for a few moments before he started it back up and drove away. He didn't know who had killed Tim and the others or why, and he wasn't going to trust going in his house and have someone kill him or Jeryca.

"I'm going to get a room for a few nights until shit is figured out. I'm going to stop at Walmart real fast so I can get a video player. I need to review those tapes," Orlando said, informing Jeryca of his change in plans. They were going to get a room in the city because anyone who knew Orlando knew he would never get a room in the city. He wasn't going to take any chances at all. "Change up my routine on they ass, baby," he said as he gave Jeryca's knee a little squeeze.

Orlando stopped at Walmart and then headed to the hotel. Once they were in the room, he sat down on a chair and leaned his head back, rubbing his face. "All right, let me hook this thang up."

Once it was hooked up to the television, Orlando popped a tape in and pushed play. He watched every move that each of the intruders made. He wanted to see if there was any familiarity in their moves, body style, or voice. Although it was faint, he felt he knew who the guys were. He just couldn't put his finger on it. They watched up until the point when the assailant shot Tim.

"Go back, Orlando!" Jeryca shouted, pointing to the screen.

"What is it?" he asked.

"Go back to where the man pointed the gun at Tim," she instructed.

Orlando did as she asked, and once he was at the scene, she asked him to pause the tape.

"Blow it up," she said. "Now look at the man's wrist area. Do you see what it says? It's 'Tiffany.' I know who that is. It's got to be Toby and Thad. I remember seeing the tattoo several times."

"Oh, shit! Girl, you are right! That's where I know that voice from. Mothafucka! They tried me like that! Okay. Okay, I got they ass!" Orlando yelled.

He paced back and forth and ranted for about ten minutes until Jeryca grabbed him and wrapped her arms around him. It was his breaking point. He cried as he embraced her tightly and the two stood holding one another.

Orlando finally let Jeryca go and called Sergio, who seemed to have been waiting for his call. "What you got for us?" Sergio asked.

"I was watching the tape, and me and my girl know who killed Tim," Orlando replied.

"Tell me who did this!" Sergio screamed.

"Man, it was Thad and Toby Royster," Orlando said, full of emotion.

"It was who? Do them bastards know what they have done? How do you know this for sure?" Sergio asked.

"It's all caught on tape. I recognize the voice, but my girl recognized the tattoo," Orlando explained.

"So your girl is associated with them somehow?" Sergio asked.

"She used to date Thad Royster, sir," Orlando replied.

"I need proof that those bastards killed Tim. We will be flying in tomorrow. I want to see this tape, and I want your girlfriend to prove to me that Thad and Toby are the men in the video," Sergio said angrily.

"All right, I will see you all tomorrow," Orlando said, before hanging up.

"Orlando, why are those guys so interested in Tim's murderers?" Jeryca inquired.

"Jeryca, Tim's father was their cousin, and he died pulling a job for the Colombians. They promised Tim's mother that they would always be there for him and keep him as safe as possible and out of this game. Tim never sold on a corner nor was he involved in any runs. At least, that was supposed to be the plan. I think they are about to wreak havoc on your boys, and if they don't, I promise you I will," Orlando vowed.

Jeryca knew that he was serious. She had to respect that about him. That was true loyalty in her opinion. She laid her head on his shoulder, and the two drifted off to sleep.

Somewhere in the middle of the night, Jeryca and Orlando retired to the bedroom and fell back to sleep. When they awoke again, it was nine o'clock in the morning, and Jeryca's cell phone was ringing.

As she looked to see who was calling her, Orlando rolled over and kissed her on the cheek. He got up to shower. Jeryca answered her phone. "Hey, Mom."

"What happened to you all yesterday?" she asked.

"Well, we got caught up in a serious situation, and we couldn't make it."

"Serious enough where you couldn't pick up the phone and call me? I mean, really, Jeryca, this is ridiculous and becoming an ugly habit of yours. I know you got your issues with me, but Pam needs you," Sheila Mebane stormed.

"Mother, if you must know, Orlando's close friend was murdered yesterday, and we spent most of our time at the police department!" Jeryca yelled.

There was a brief silence. "You still could've called, Jeryca."

"Oh, my God! Are you fucking deaf? Listen, I don't have time for this right now, so I will talk to you later," Jeryca shouted and hung up.

A few seconds later, her phone rang again. "What, Mom?" she shouted aggressively.

"While you sitting there yelling at me, your sister is in the hospital. Her appendix burst and they have her in emergency surgery. They say that it's very serious and I figured you would want to know!" Sheila cried.

Jeryca sat upright in the bed. "What? When did this happen?" she asked with a concerned tone.

"She woke up complaining about her side hurting, and she started vomiting. I didn't think it was anything too serious, so I gave her some Pepto-Bismol, but when the pain got worse, I called 911. We are here at Brooklyn Hospital Center on the second floor, in the surgery waiting area," Sheila stated.

"We? Who is we, Mom?" Jeryca asked.

"Paul is here. I called him to let him know what was going on," she answered.

"Why would you do that? He ain't never cared about her," Jeryca shouted.

"He is her father, and he deserved to know. Are you coming down here?" Sheila asked.

"Yes. Let me get a shower and get dressed. I will be there, I promise," Jeryca said, before hanging up.

When she turned around, Orlando was standing there, looking at her. "Is everything all right?"

"Yes. Well, no. My sister is in the hospital, and I need to get down there as soon as possible," she replied.

"Listen, I know it's none of my business but, Jeryca, you shouldn't talk to your mom like that. She is the reason you are here, and you should respect her for that if nothing else."

"I just don't know how. I don't respect anything about her, baby. She isn't the kind of woman I ever wanted to look up to," Jeryca replied.

"I know, but you should try to be a little less mouthy. That's all I'm saying, okay?" Orlando asked.

"All right, I will try it your way," she said.

"That's all I ask," Orlando said. "Come on. Get out of this bed and get your shower so we can get going. Sergio and Ramon will be in later, and I got to get with Tim's mom and help her out as much as I can," he told her.

"All right, I'm getting up," Jeryca said, smiling.

As she got up, he noticed she only had on a pair of lace panties and a tank top. As she waltzed by him, she smiled, knowing he was watching her.

"Lord have mercy, girl," he whispered.

Chapter Two

Orlando and Jeryca arrived at the hospital forty-five minutes after she had hung up with her mom. Orlando walked her up to the second floor, and when they walked into the waiting room, Jeryca's mom jumped up and grabbed Jeryca, hugging her and crying.

When she let her go, she looked at Orlando and extended her hand. "Hi, I'm Sheila Mebane, Jeryca's mother."

"Nice to meet you, Ms. Mebane. I'm Orlando, Jeryca's boyfriend."

"Oh, okay. I'm sorry to hear about your friend. I don't know what's going on in this world today. People are killing other people like it's nothing!" Sheila said, shaking her head.

"Yes, ma'am, it's quite sad. I want to let you know that my prayers are with you and your family. I hope Pam pulls through this. I'm sure if she has any of her sister's fight, she will," Orlando said.

"Thank you. Jeryca, you got you a decent man right here. I hope you don't make me regret giving you a mother's seal of approval," Sheila said, smiling at him then Jeryca.

"Where's Paul?" asked Jeryca.

"He had to leave," Sheila said and left it at that.

Orlando stayed with them for about an hour. He laughed and talked to Sheila as if he had known her for years. Jeryca smiled at the two of them and was surprised at how well her mother was behaving. Orlando excused himself and apologized for rushing off, but he swore he would call throughout the day to check in.

Jeryca walked him to the elevator and hugged him tightly. She wished she could be with him during this time, but her sister needed her more.

"I'm going to miss you, babe." Jeryca sighed.

"I'm going to miss you too," Orlando said as he looked down at Jeryca.

"Okay, bae, call me when you get time later on," she replied.

"All right, I will."

Orlando left the hospital and drove straight to Tim's mother's house. As he pulled up into the driveway, there were several cars lined up on the side of the road. People were going in and out of the house and Tim's girlfriend, Lynn, was being held up as she exited the house. She was screaming and crying, which pulled on

Orlando's heartstrings. He parked and slowly got out of the car. As he approached the steps, Lynn looked at him and reached out for him. He grabbed her hand and pulled her to him. As he embraced her, he could feel her body trembling.

He pulled back, looked her in the face, and assured her that they were going to find out who was responsible, even though he already knew.

He walked into the house, and the scene was heart wrenching. Everyone was crying, and the living room was filled with pictures of Tim. His mother was sitting in front of the television, watching the news coverage of the deaths. She wasn't saying a word to anyone. It was as if she were in a world of her own.

Orlando walked over and stood next to her. He gripped her shoulder and gave it a squeeze, letting her know he was there. She looked up at him, tears filling her eyes, and suddenly she broke down. He held her for a few minutes, and then she sat up. "I'm sorry about that. How are you doing?"

"I'm doing as well as I can be under the circumstances. Is there anything I can do while I'm here?" he asked her.

"If you can, help pull the chairs out from the garage, and set them up throughout the house and on the porch. I got to do a store run to get some food for the guests who will be arriving," she replied.

"I can handle all that. What are you going to do as far as the funeral is concerned?" Orlando asked.

"I don't want to drag this out, so I decided to have a service for him tomorrow, and I'm going to have him cremated," she explained.

"Oh, sounds good. I'm going to get started pulling those chairs out and then I'll go to the store." Orlando sighed.

"You are a good man, Orlando, and my Timmy was lucky to have a friend like you," she said sadly.

"I was the lucky one," Orlando said, before asking Tim's cousin to help him with the chairs.

After a couple of hours, Orlando had finished setting up the chairs and had gone shopping. He set everything up in the kitchen, where the food and drinks were easily accessible. He picked up his phone, about to call Jeryca, when he heard two familiar voices coming from the hallway.

He walked quickly to the hall and was happy to see Sergio and Ramon standing there. Sergio was hugging Tim's mom, and Ramon was hugging Lynn.

Finally, they spotted Orlando. "Nice of you to come," Orlando said.

"Where else would we be?" Ramon asked.

Orlando shook his head in agreement.

Sergio wrapped one arm around Orlando's neck and walked him to the front porch. "Listen, we are leaving in the morning before services begin, so we need to see that video and talk to your friend. If she can prove that Thad and Toby are responsible for all this, then we need to see that proof and rid ourselves of those bastards."

"I understand. I will go and get the video in a few minutes, and I'll call Jeryca and see if she can make time for a meeting tonight," Orlando replied.

"We do appreciate you, man," Sergio said.

Orlando went back into the house with Sergio and listened to them put the obituary together. After an hour, they all sat down to dinner. Orlando didn't stay. He told them he was going to pick up the tape and he would meet them at the hotel suite.

Orlando dialed Jeryca's number, but it went straight to voicemail. Orlando knew that it would probably be impossible to pull Jeryca away from her sister, so he would explain to Ramon and Sergio that they might not meet Jeryca before they left.

Jeryca had spent most of the day by her sister's side. The doctor had informed them that the surgery was a success, although it was touch and go for a while. Pam had awakened thirty minutes after leaving the recovery room, and Jeryca never felt more relieved.

They talked for a little while, and Pam begged Jeryca to stay with her for the night. Jeryca agreed. She wasn't going anywhere until she knew that Pam was definitely okay.

Jeryca decided to go to the hospital chapel and say a prayer for Pam. En route, she passed a room that was closed off with glass walls, and what she saw caught her attention. Brenda was lying in the bed with tubes running out of her body. She had heard that Brenda was still alive and that she was in a vegetative state, but to see her with her own two eyes made it surreal.

She reflected on the day that Dana shot Brenda. Jeryca felt that Dana overreacted a bit during the robbery, but then again, she had recognized who Jeryca was immediately.

Jeryca felt awful for the things that had transpired through the months, and in her mind, there was only one person really to blame: Dana!

Dana was going to pay for all that had happened, and Jeryca was certain that she would also. However, she was going to watch Dana fall, before it was her own time to pay karma.

Chapter Three

Current Day

Detectives Rone and Harris sat in the back of the conference room and waited for Detective Lisa Moore to finish briefing the officers on Timothy Vaughan's murder case. Detective Rone wasn't on the murder case, but when he learned that Jeryca Mebane was involved, he had to get the details.

There were too many deaths surrounding Jeryca Mebane and Dana Crisp. He had to find out what was going on. He had a strange woman calling him, informing him of all these crimes that Dana Crisp was involved in, yet he had no proof that any crime was committed. He had spoken to Debra, and she assured him that she was okay, so there was no crime there. Just a few days ago, the woman called again, informing him that Dana may have been involved in the murder of Keith Turner, but again, no evidence was found. He didn't want to think that Dana could be involved in those murders, but there were a lot of bodies piling up. She and her friends were connected in one way or another, and he was going to get to the bottom of it.

As Lisa Moore concluded her conference and walked toward the exit, Detective Rone approached her. "Excuse me, Lisa, I would like to know if I can assist you on this case. I think this may have some bearing on a murder case that I have been investigating."

"And what case might that be, Detective Rone?" she asked.

"Farrah Walker's murder case," he answered.

"I thought that case had been solved and closed, Detective," she said, looking at him curiously.

"Yeah, it was, but recent evidence has been placed before me that may mean I'll need to reopen her case. The people involved in your investigation are connected to mine as well," he replied.

"Oh, yeah? And who might that be?" she asked.

"Jeryca Mebane, for starters," he said flatly.

"Oh, really? Well, I think that we definitely need to discuss a few things. Let me grab my keys and we can talk in my office," she said.

"Sounds good to me," Detective Rone said, as he looked at Detective Harris and smiled.

While Detective Moore went to retrieve her keys, Detective Harris looked at Detective Rone, frowning. "There isn't any new evidence in the Walker case. Why did you say that?"

"Because I need to do everything in my power to make sure that whoever's been calling me isn't actually telling me the truth about these murders," Detective Rone replied.

Detective Harris looked at him and shrugged his shoulders. "Okay, let's go."

Wednesday night, Brittany, Deondre, Minx, and Dana pulled up at the warehouse at 10:00 p.m. They decided that it was time to take care of Debra and move on. Dana felt that it was long overdue, but Brittany kept prolonging it.

Brittany was the first to get out of the car, with Dana on her heels. The two men were in a separate truck and lingered behind, removing several items from the truck.

Brittany unlocked the warehouse and walked in. She immediately went to the room where Debra was being kept. She had a feeling that she was making the wrong decision, but everybody involved felt that Debra should die, and she had to roll with the majority.

"Let's do this so we can leave. It's too late to try to change your mind," Dana whispered.

"I'm not changing my mind. Just back off, Dana!" Brittany growled.

"Don't get mad at me. I ain't did shit to you. Just do this so I can get the fuck away from you," Dana muttered, glaring at Brittany.

Brittany smiled. "Dana, you just don't know when to quit. But I'm telling you, quit trying me."

Dana smiled back but said nothing. She couldn't wait to finish this and be on her way. She decided that once the Debra situation was taken care of, she wasn't fucking with any of them again. It was time to move on, and that's exactly what she was going to do.

A few seconds later, Deondre and Minx walked up. "What's going on? Why are y'all just standing out here?" Minx asked.

Dana stepped back and waved her hand toward Brittany. "Ask her."

"Man, if you don't get in there and fucking kill that bitch, Brittany . . . We ain't got time for no bullshit," Deondre said, clearly aggravated.

"All right, damn. I'm going," Brittany replied. She opened the door to the room and turned the lights on. There was a strong odor of urine and feces in the air.

"Oh, my. Damn!" Dana said, covering her nose.

Deondre waved his hand through the air, furiously fanning. "Eww, fuck! It stinks like fuck in here. Let's get this over with!"

Debra was so weak that she could hardly hold her head up. The light severely hurt her eyes, due to being in the dark for so many days. She hadn't eaten or had water in a while.

Brittany looked at how sunken in her eyes were and how thin her face was. It was shocking to her that Debra wasn't already dead. She decided to make it quick because, in her opinion, Debra had suffered enough.

"Y'all get everything ready so I can do this, and we can get the hell out of here," Brittany ordered.

After they had filled a crate with weights and put plastic on the floor with thick chain links laid out, Brittany walked over to Debra with a heavy heart and stood behind her.

"I'm sorry that it had to come to this, Debra. I really am," she whispered. Brittany wrapped the rope around Debra's neck and strangled the remaining life out of her.

When it was over, Deondre and Minx dragged her lifeless body out of the chair, placed it on the plastic, and wrapped her up in it. Then they rolled her body back over into a thick wool blanket and secured it with the chain links. They lifted her body into the crate, which would be taken to the ocean and disposed of. Minx had a friend who owned a boat, and he was going to loan it to him for what he assumed was a fishing trip.

It took Brittany and Dana a few hours to clean up the room, and it was done in an awkward silence. Deondre and Minx had left for their "fishing trip" and were going to call Brittany and Dana once everything was taken care of.

Dana was ready for Zack and Orlando to return so she could get her cut from the robbery they pulled on Thad. She had wanted revenge on them, but she never imagined that things would go as far as they had. She was disgusted by everything that she had done. She had always been a woman who worked for what she wanted, and she had allowed her hurt, anger, and greed to lead her to where she presently was.

Orlando called Jeryca Thursday morning and asked her what she had planned for the weekend. He explained to her that he had been summoned to South Florida for a meeting and he needed her to tag along. Not only was she being summoned, he also felt that she could learn a lot and gain a lot by riding with him. She had potential, in his opinion, to be a trustworthy rider chick. He liked her a lot, so when she accepted his invitation, he got so excited that his dick got hard. He wanted to fuck Jeryca, but he was interested in more than just pussy. However, if she chose to give it up on their trip, he was going to put it down.

He hung up after talking with her for almost an hour, explaining that Sergio and Ramon needed to see evidence that Thad and Toby were responsible for the robbery and that Toby was the triggerman. After he got off the phone with Jeryca, he relaxed for a bit, and then he began laying out the plans for their trip. He had called Zack also, because Ramon had taken a liking to him and requested that he come along as well. Zack's plans to take over the East Coast appealed to the Colombians, and they were going to see how things played out after the situation with Thad was dealt with.

Thad and Toby had fucked up killing Tim. Tim was a very important man to Sergio and Ramon. He was family to them, and they were close. They were disgusted by what they saw on the video, and they told Orlando that they were going to let him know where he was going to meet them. They would use that time to discuss some things and drop off a few diamonds to help him get his revenge on Thad.

Orlando had to thank God that he wasn't there when the robbery went down because he was sure they would've killed him also. He missed Tim a lot. He was his right-hand man, and they had been cool for years. He was like his little brother, and now he was gone.

"Why the fuck would they kill Tim?" Orlando muttered aloud.

Orlando had planned to leave the game completely after the last lick, but he couldn't let Thad and his boys get away with killing Tim. Those bastards deserved everything that Sergio and Ramon had planned for them. He really wanted them to keep one of them alive so they could see and feel all the loss they were going to take. Maybe afterward, they could kill them. He was going to pose that question to the Colombians once he got to Florida.

Orlando's cell phone began to ring, but the caller ID was blocked. He ignored it and continued setting up their plans online. A beeping noise sounded, alerting him that he had a voicemail. He decided to check it once he finished booking their hotel reservations.

Once he finished making the reservations for himself and Jeryca, he called Zack and told him to go on and make his reservations and get his ticket. He gave Zack the hotel number and the time that he would need to meet them at the airport. Sergio had made preparations for his private jet to fly them down to Florida. Ramon and Sergio were very decent guys until a person crossed them.

Orlando looked at Tim's obituary, sat down, and stared at it for a few moments. He couldn't believe that his friend was gone. Tim was always by his side through everything, and he felt alone. Jeryca had been by his side through it all, except the funeral. He understood that she had family obligations with her sister. Jeryca had texted him throughout the two days that she was gone and he appreciated her a lot. He understood and respected that she was dealing with her own family issues.

Thursday afternoon, Jeryca sat next to her sister in her hospital bed and grabbed her hand. "I love you, sis, and I want you to remember that, okay?"

"I know you love me. Why are you talking like I'm not going to see you again?" Pam said quietly, looking in Jeryca's eyes.

"I just want you to know how I feel. That's all, sis," Jeryca replied, smiling. "But I am leaving tomorrow for a few days, and I don't have any choice in the matter. I will be back as soon as I finish with my business," she finished.

"You aren't doing anything illegal, are you?" Pam asked, frowning.

"No, I'm not. It's just a business meeting," Jeryca explained.

"Oh, okay. I will be all right until you come back," Pam said.

Jeryca honestly didn't know what the next few weeks held for her. She had spent the whole night thinking of how things had changed, and what she could do to fix a few things in her life. She wasn't going to rest until she got revenge on all those responsible for Farrah's death.

She had been calling and checking up on Shirley and Travis, and they seemed to be slowly getting back on their feet. Travis was in counseling, along with his grandmother. Shirley confessed to her that she didn't know if she was going to be able to care for Travis long-term. She was too old to be raising a young boy his age. Jeryca knew she was throwing hints to her, but Jeryca also knew that she wasn't the right person to raise Travis either. She suggested that Karen be named his legal guardian. Shirley agreed that Karen might be the ideal person. She promised to keep Jeryca posted on how they were doing from time to time, and she would allow her to see Travis whenever possible.

Jeryca spent Friday morning kicking it with Pam. She hadn't left her sister's side since she got there, but it was time for her to leave and go meet with Orlando. She hugged and kissed her mother, and promised her sister that she wouldn't be gone long and that they'd go shopping when she returned.

Her mother looked at her and smiled. "Jeryca, I do like your friend. He seems to be very good for you."

Jeryca smiled and thanked her mom for giving her the green light to date Orlando, even though it wasn't needed. Jeryca was going to see him regardless.

Chapter Four

Arrival in Palm Beach, Florida

As soon as Jeryca got off the jet in Palm Beach, Florida, she was in awe of the beautiful scenery. Orlando smiled as he watched her facial expressions change. He grabbed her hand and tugged at her gently. "Come on, babe, let's go and get checked into the hotel, and once we are unpacked, we can enjoy all the beautiful sights there are to take in."

Jeryca smiled and walked alongside Orlando, thankful that she had him in her life. She had never been outside of New York, so she was going to make the most of the trip. Zack was already at the limousine that Orlando had arranged to meet them and take them around town. Zack wished that he could've invited Dana along, but he was there for business, and he didn't want Dana involved on that particular trip.

The three of them got into the limo and were taken to the hotel. Jeryca looked out the window, feeling relaxed as they drove past the strip. There were boutiques lined up on each side of the road, but when she caught a glimpse of the hotel they were going to stay in, she was floored.

As they pulled into the parking lot and stopped in front of the building, there was an attendant waiting for them. He helped them out of the car, gathered their luggage, and escorted them to the front desk. While Orlando and Zack signed in and retrieved the room keys, Jeryca admired how clean and refined the hotel was.

"This is going to be a weekend to remember!" she murmured to herself.

"Come on, Sweet J, let's get unpacked so we can go and do a little sightseeing before it gets too dark," Orlando said, as he walked over and placed his hand on the small of her back.

"All right. I'm all for that," she replied.

After the two unpacked and relaxed for an hour, Orlando called down to the concierge and asked if they could have a car meet them in the front of the hotel in forty-five minutes. He was going to enjoy the rest of the day shopping and walking the beach with his newfound love.

Before they left, Jeryca took a shower, and Orlando took that opportunity to call Ramon.

"We are here. I got us a room at the Eau Palm Beach Resort & Spa. I'm going to relax today and get with y'all tomorrow," Orlando said.

"Zack is already over here, and we have discussed a few things. I like him, and I think we gon' do great business together," Ramon replied.

"Oh, is he? Well, I guess he didn't want to wait on me. Zack and I are here for two different reasons, so y'all handle your business and I will meet y'all tomorrow. Will that work for you guys?" Orlando asked.

"Yes, that's fine. And I'm glad Jeryca could make it. We need her to tell us all she knows about Thad and Toby. My top hitters will be here also, and trust me, they are ready to take care of our pests," Ramon replied.

"All right, I look forward to seeing y'all tomorrow," Orlando said, before hanging up.

Once Jeryca was out of the shower and dressed, they left and took in the sights. Orlando took her shopping, took her to the beach, and then he took her to the number one spot to eat, Leopard Lounge & Restaurant. Jeryca ate Greek food for the first time, and she enjoyed it.

There was a live band playing, and after they ate dinner, they danced the night away. They headed back to the hotel at eleven o'clock, when the restaurant closed. Jeryca felt as if she were floating. Orlando made her feel so good, and she felt it was about time to show him how much she appreciated him.

Once they were back at the hotel, Orlando took a shower, and when he came out, Jeryca was sitting on the bed. "Come on over here and let me give you a massage."

He walked over and sat down next to Jeryca. "Lie down," she whispered after she took his shirt off.

Orlando was quite a bit older than Jeryca. He was thirty-five whereas she was only twenty-three. He was nicely built, but he had a small gut. He had a close cut with sideburns that met a thinly trimmed goatee. He had streaks of gray in his goatee, which made him look refined in Jeryca's eyes. His eyes were light brown and almost smoky looking. He was five foot ten, and his smile was almost scary because he seemed serious all the time.

Orlando stretched out across the king-sized bed, and he was amazed at how soft Jeryca's hands felt on his back. She had straddled him and was giving him one of the best massages he had received in a long time.

As he started getting relaxed, she suddenly stopped. "Don't move. I'll be right back," she whispered.

She walked into the bathroom, and as he lay there, he couldn't help but wonder what she had planned. After about three minutes, Jeryca returned, wearing a short red lace nightgown. He was turned on instantly. "Oh, my God. Those legs, girl, damn. You don't know what you do to me," he groaned as he reached for her and pulled her on top of him.

"Uh-uh. I'm in control tonight," Jeryca said, as she moved his hands off her waist and placed them above his head. "No matter what I do, you cannot move your hands from above your head."

"Jeryca, you know you ain't got to do this!" He moaned as he felt her lips on his thigh.

She looked up and smiled. "I know I don't. I'm ready, and I want to do this."

He sighed as her kisses traveled up to his nuts. She sucked his balls: right side first, then left. As her lips traveled upward and she licked the side of his dick, he sucked in a deep breath and grasped the pillow. Once she reached the head of his dick, she looked him in his face, and as their eyes met, she slowly sucked his dick, taking him in her mouth inch by inch. Orlando moaned as she began increasing speed.

As he was about to cum, he jerked back and sat up. "I'm not 'bout to cum like that. You gon' sit on this dick."

As he grabbed her hands and pulled her on top of him, he slid down so that his mouth could reach her breasts. He sucked on her nipples and ran his tongue around them repeatedly, which drove Jeryca crazy. Jeryca and Orlando paused for a moment, but only long enough for him to grab a condom off the night table beside the bed. Jeryca took the condom, and once she placed it on his super-hard dick, she straddled him. She slid slowly down on his dick and moved around, increasing speed.

He thrust upward, meeting her, and as he gripped her ass, she let out a loud moan. She had never experienced sex like that. Orlando grabbed her head, lifted up slightly, and began kissing her fiercely. She started moving faster and faster until both of them came. To Jeryca's surprise, Orlando held her in place and continued moving inside her. She felt him getting hard again. He flipped her over on her back, grabbed her feet, and moved them so she could wrap them around his back. The two hit a rhythm, and he made love to her for a second time, but it was more intimate.

Afterward, they showered together and went to sleep. For the second time, Jeryca slept in Orlando's arms, and she knew that she was exactly where she needed to be.

***

The next morning, they were awakened by a knock on the door. Orlando jumped up, grabbed his gun from the drawer, and walked quietly to the door. "Who is it?" he asked.

"Man, it's me, Zack! Open the door, damn!" he said, laughing.

Orlando opened the door halfway. "Man, give us 'bout ten minutes. We gon' get dressed and meet you down in the lobby."

"All right, playa!" Zack said, smiling at Orlando. Orlando waved him off and shut the door.

Jeryca was already in the bathroom brushing her teeth. Orlando walked in and stood behind her, looking at their reflection in the mirror. "Even with all that gunk in your mouth, we still look good together. Don't we?" he asked.

Jeryca rinsed her mouth out and then stood up and smiled as she saw how good they truly looked. She turned to face him. His arms immediately went around her, and she whispered, "I'm glad I got you."

The two kissed and finished getting dressed, ready to meet Sergio and Ramon. Jeryca had her own personal agenda for meeting with them.

The three of them were finally in the limousine, heading to meet the Colombians. Jeryca was nervous as hell, but she wasn't going to show it.

Orlando glanced over at her repeatedly and gave her hand a small squeeze to let her know everything was going to be okay. She smiled and gazed into his eyes, trying to assure him that she was okay.

Once they pulled up, Zack was the first one out of the car. Once again, Jeryca was awestruck at the sight. They were at an ocean-side condo that sat up off the sand and was made out of the most beautiful wood and stone material she had ever seen. The steps that they had to walk up to get to the door were rough granite.

It was lovely. There were five men walking around the condo outside, and each one of the out-of-towners was patted down before they were allowed to enter. As big as the condo was, Jeryca was shocked by the layout inside. It was nothing like she expected. The inside of the condo was clean, but its layout was simple. There wasn't anything extravagant about it. She thought that Colombians lived luxuriously wherever they were. At least, that's what she had seen in the movies.

Zack sat on a couch next to a lovely black woman. Her hair was done in a small, bushy style. Jeryca had to admire a woman who was all natural. Her eyes were dark brown with long, thick lashes. She had full lips, and her cheekbones were high. Zack was engrossed in conversation with her instantly.

There was a second woman sitting in a wing-back chair, and she looked mean. She didn't smile at all, and just as Jeryca was taking in her appearance, the woman was, in turn, checking her out. She was a white woman with blond hair and blue eyes, and she had a piercing above her eye. She wore a black tank top and blue khakis with black boots. As hot as it was in Palm Beach, Jeryca imagined that she had to be hot as hell with all that on.

Orlando sat down on a love seat, and Jeryca joined him. The white woman got up and walked toward the back. When she returned, she was followed by two men. They appeared to Jeryca to have Latin features. They both had long black hair, and their skin was tanned. Orlando imme-diately stood up and walked over to greet the two men.

"How are you Ramon, Sergio?" he asked them as he shook their hands.

"We are good, thanks. This must be Jeryca," Ramon said, as he walked over to her with his hand extended.

"Yes, I am," Jeryca said, as she stood to shake his hand.

"No, please, sit back down. I'm glad that you could come on such short notice. Orlando told us that he was going to take you sightseeing. What do you think of Palm Beach?" he asked her as he sat down beside her.

"I love it. Everything is beautiful here. This is my first time down South, and I'm loving the atmosphere already," she said, smiling.

"Well, maybe you and Orlando can visit South America one day. I'm from Uruguay, and I'm sure you would love it there," Ramon said, smiling. "Zack, what's up, my man? I'm glad you are here. I enjoyed our little chat yesterday and I know we can make some big moves," Ramon said.

He then turned his attention to Sergio and Orlando. "Let's see the tape again and see how this beautiful creature can prove that the guy is Toby Royster. Get the video and put it in the player," Ramon instructed the black woman who was seated next to Zack.

She immediately got up and grabbed the case that Orlando handed her. She turned on the television and popped the video in the player. As they watched the tape, Jeryca glanced at the two Colombian men and saw the anger in their faces. She quickly looked back at the screen when she saw Sergio looking back at her. Once they got to the part where the shooter outstretched his arm to shoot Tim, Jeryca spoke. "Stop the tape right there. Can you enlarge it a bit?"

After it was enlarged, she pointed to the tattoo on the guy's wrist. "You see that word? It's 'Tiffany,' and that's Toby's wife's name." She dug into her purse and pulled two photos from her wallet. "This is Toby and Thad together when we first started dating. You can see the tattoo clearly on his arm. This is another picture of him and Tiffany, with Thad and me, and she is happily showing off the tattoo. That's all the proof I really have. I know that's Toby and Thad together. I don't know who else was involved, but your shooter is this man right here," she said, pointing to Toby.

Everyone sat quietly at first, and then Sergio spoke. "That's all the proof we need. Thank you," he said, looking at Jeryca. He stood up and motioned for Orlando, Zack, and the other two women to accompany him to the back room.

Once they all relocated, Jeryca smiled and said quietly to herself, "Phase one complete."

Chapter Five

Meanwhile, back in Brooklyn, Dana was at the shop getting her hair stylishly cut. She decided it was time for a new look for the new her. She had found an apartment in Massachusetts and managed to find a job as well. Everything was working out just as she wanted. Zack had informed her that he would be returning Monday and they would split up the money from the robbery. That worked out perfectly for Dana. She hated having to uproot her life from the Bronx, but she had to do what she had to do. Things had gotten way out of control, and she didn't know whom she could trust.

She planned to leave two weeks from that day, and she vowed she would never return. She hadn't talked to Stephanie or Jeryca about her decision, and she doubted she would. She had to make the change with no one knowing where she was going.

Jeryca was enjoying her time in Florida. She had actually been able to penetrate the rough exteriors of the women who were Sergio and Ramon's top hitters, as they called them.

The black woman was Desiree, and the white, mean-looking one was Valerie. She wasn't as mean as Jeryca initially thought she was. They were both definitely team players. Jeryca was focused on her own devious plan, and they would come in handy. She was going to be the top bitch at Orlando's side. She was going to run the East Coast with her man. She just had to move a few pieces around to make it happen.

Sergio and Ramon both told her that if there was a way they could repay her for helping them pinpoint Tim's murderer, they had her. Jeryca knew exactly what she wanted, and she was going to ask to have a private sit-down with them, and of course, Orlando. It was time for her to make her move as well.

She walked into the bedroom area of the suite, lay down across Orlando's body, and started rubbing her hands up and down his chest. "Orlando, can you call Sergio and let him know I would like to discuss something with them, please? I want all of us on board, but it's going to take some talking to get Zack on board."

"What kind of plan are you concocting, J?" he asked, smiling.

"I'm not saying until we are all together. That way I can see everyone's reaction to it at one time," she said.

"Girl, you are crazy. Give me those lips, though," he said, as he rubbed his finger over them.

Jeryca sighed as she sucked his finger. She then straddled him and kissed him. He grabbed her hips and started rotating his hips against her body. She felt his dick growing, and she smiled. She looked down at him and whispered, "You gonna call them tomorrow, right?"

"Yes, I am. Now take them pajamas off!"

The next day, Jeryca spoke with Sergio and Ramon, and they agreed to provide her with the things she needed to finalize the plan she had devised. Although Zack wasn't 100 percent okay with the plan, he went along with it, due to the amount of money that he stood to gain.

Two days later, Jeryca, Orlando, and Zack boarded a plane heading back to Brooklyn, New York. Five of Sergio and Ramon's top hitters accompanied them, including Valerie and Desiree, who were in charge of the all-male crew. They had one mission, which was to bring back the man who killed Tim. Sergio didn't want them to kill him, because he wanted to do it, but only after they tortured him. Thad, they would deal with in an entirely different way.

"Ay, y'all, we ain't gon' have time to play around. We got three days to do everything we came here to do," Desiree explained, and then looked at Jeryca. "I'm going to need you to show me where Toby lives and where their warehouse is located."

"I got you. We can do that as soon as we touch down. Then I got to take care of a few things myself," Jeryca replied.

"All right, so we all clear?" Desiree asked.

After everyone said yes, Valerie spoke. "Orlando, you and Zack will need to go on and get us the guns that we need as soon as possible. We going in hard and exiting quick. Ramon has arranged for Tim's cousin to get us a truck, a van, and a car, which will be used for different things. We can't mess this up!"

Once they touched down, a man was there waiting for them. Jeryca and the two women got into the car, Zack and Orlando got into the truck, and the three Colombian triggermen got into the van. They were to follow Zack and Orlando to Zack's house. Orlando wasn't sure if the cops were still watching his house and he refused to go there with Sergio's guys with him.

Dana was lying on her couch talking to Brittany. They hadn't been talking a lot since their blowup. Dana didn't trust her at all, but she wasn't going to write any of them completely off until she got her cut from the robbery. In the middle of her phone call, Zack called in.

"Hold on, Brittany. This is Zack calling now," Dana said, before clicking over. "Hello?" she said.

"Hey, how are you doing?" Zack asked.

"I'm good and you?" she replied.

"I'm tired, but it's cool. Look, we are going to meet up at the warehouse over on Jackson Street to split up some of this stuff. We are leaving again in the morning, and Orlando and I figured we could get some of this stuff off before we leave. We were able to sell a few of the guns and dope. We moved all the stuff to our new location this morning, because of all the issues with the police. Orlando don't want all this falling back on him," Zack explained.

"I thought you were coming in on Monday," Dana replied.

"We had a change of plans. We got so much to do, you know," Zack said quietly.

"Oh, okay. Well, I'm on the phone with Brittany now. Do you want me to tell her?" Dana asked.

"No. Get off the phone with her so I can call and tell her. You can call Stephanie to let her know, and try to be here in 'bout thirty minutes to an hour. Ay, you won't see my car there. I had to get a rental for a few days," he said.

"All right, I got you. I'm getting ready now. Talk to you in a few," Dana said, before hanging up.

She clicked back over to Brittany. "Ay, Zack 'bout to call you, so I'm going to let you go."

"All right. Yeah, he beeping in now," Brittany said.

When Dana got off the phone, she dialed Stephanie's number but got no answer. She called a few more times, and finally, Dana gave up. She grabbed her keys and walked out the door.

Friday evening, Stephanie was sitting at Robin's apartment, waiting for her to get home. She had been waiting there for almost an hour and a half, and she still hadn't gotten there. She knew Robin had gotten off work, because she stopped by there first.

She walked into Robin's bedroom and sat on the bed. She looked around the room, and she saw a pack of matches with RAMADA INN & SUITES engraved on it. She suddenly felt sick. Chris had told her at the Oasis that he was staying there and she had the room number.

She immediately ran out of the apartment and jumped into her mother's green sedan. She only allowed her a few hours with the car, and here she was wasting time by chasing after Robin. She prayed that she was wrong and that Robin wouldn't have betrayed her like that, but her gut told her that Robin had.

She arrived at the hotel and got directions to where she could find Chris's room. Once there, she could hear a lot of moaning coming from inside the room. Her heart fell to the ground. She stood frozen for a minute, but then anger set in and she started banging on the door.

She heard a lot of moving around and then she heard Chris yell, "Who is it?"

"It's Stephanie. Open the door, Chris."

There was a brief silence, but he finally opened the door. Stephanie's heart began to pound wildly in her chest as she saw Robin standing in the room with a sheet thrown around her.

Robin kept looking angrily at Chris. "Why would you open the fucking door?" Robin yelled.

Stephanie flew at Chris, fists balled up and swinging. She cursed at him and then she flew at Robin. She grabbed her by her hair and slung her to the floor. Chris pulled her off Robin. "Chill the fuck out! These folks are going to call the police, and I'm not getting kicked out because of you."

"Fuck you! Fuck both of you! How could you do this to me?" she asked, looking at Robin.

Robin turned her head, unable to look at Stephanie. When she looked back, she shook her head. "I just wanted to see what he was about. That night at the club, I saw how you two looked at one another. I would've been a fool not to see the chemistry you still had. I didn't want to be left out if you picked back up with him. We can all be in this together," Robin said, as her eyes pleaded with Stephanie to understand.

Stephanie looked at Robin, her heart aching. "I would never have gone back to Chris, no matter what I felt, 'cause my love for you was stronger. But now, Robin, you are in the same boat as him. I don't ever want to see either of you again."

Stephanie walked out the door and ran out of the hotel. She couldn't believe that Robin had hurt her like that. As she cranked up her car, her phone beeped. She looked at it and saw four missed calls from Dana. She turned her phone off. She didn't want to talk to anyone at all.

"I'm done with love. Now it's all about me!" she whispered to herself. She decided right then that Chris and Robin were going to hate that they ever screwed her over.

Back at the hotel, Robin stared at Chris, fuming. "Why would you do that? I thought you understood that I didn't want her to find out like this."

Chris looked at her. "Listen, get your shit on and get out. You have served your purpose."

Robin felt betrayed. "You planned this, didn't you? You wanted her to find out. This was never about getting with me. This was all about getting even with Stephanie. I feel so stupid!" Robin cried.

"Well, could you feel stupid while you're walking out of here? I got shit to do," he replied nonchalantly.

After Robin got dressed, she walked to her car and dialed Stephanie's number. It went straight to voicemail. When she got into her car, she broke down, sobbing uncontrollably. She knew she had messed up with Stephanie, and all for a taste of some dick. She loved Stephanie and didn't know how she was going to go on without her. What she did was foolish, but Stephanie had to forgive her.

As she pulled off, she saw Chris walking out. She wanted to run him over, but she scrapped that thought from her mind. She rode a few minutes and then she started hearing a weird sound coming from her car. She slowed down a bit, but the sound got louder. She pulled over once she got to Citgo, and she saw that her rear right tire was flat.

"What the fuck else can happen?" she yelled.

It took the tow truck an hour to pull up. They helped her change her tire and Robin was on her way again. Once at home and in her bedroom, Robin threw herself on her bed. She wondered how Stephanie knew she was at Chris's. She sat up and looked around and then her eyes fell on the matchbook that was on her nightstand.

"What the hell?" She sighed. She didn't smoke, so how had those matches gotten there? Suddenly it dawned on her: Chris had stopped by earlier that day claiming he needed to use the restroom, which ended up being an hour-long stay. He had left those matches, knowing that Stephanie would find them. She had really played herself. Robin lay on the bed and cried herself to sleep.

Dana arrived at the warehouse that Zack had instructed her to go to. She saw two cars in the parking lot and figured one was the rental car that Zack had said he'd gotten.

She exited the car and walked to the rear of the warehouse where the lights were on. When she entered, she called out for Zack. There was no answer. As she walked farther inside, she suddenly heard a noise behind her, and as she turned, someone hit her across the head and knocked her out.

Friday night, Tiffany and Toby were having dinner when there was a light knock at the door.

"Who is it?" Toby said once he was close up on the door.

"It's Jeryca! I need to talk to you about Keith. I tried to call Thad, but his phone went straight to voicemail. It's important," she said.

Toby stalled for a second, but he was curious as to what Jeryca had to say. He unlocked the door, and before he could open it all the way, he was pushed backward, and a gun was immediately thrown in his face.

"Go check the house and see if anyone else is here," Valerie told one of the guys standing to her left.

He and another guy walked through the house with their guns pulled.

"Jeryca, what the fuck are you doing? You know Thad is going to flip out about this," Toby said.

"Thad is the least of my worries. Just shut your mouth up!" Jeryca said as she walked by him.

Valerie pushed Toby into the living room and forced him to sit down on the couch. A few minutes later, he heard Tiffany yelling.

"Don't touch her, motherfucker!" he yelled, struggling to get up.

Desiree quickly intervened and pointed her .45-cal at his temple. "Boy, I think you need to settle down. They ain't doing shit to her yet."

Toby looked up at Desiree. "What you mean, yet? You aren't going to fuck with her, bitch!"

Desiree laughed. "You are right. I'm not."

Zack and Orlando walked into the house and headed toward the living room, where they heard Desiree's voice.

"Hey, Toby, that must be the beautiful Tiffany we've heard so much about," Zack said, looking at her as they pushed her into a chair across from Toby.

"Get them tied up and tape their mouths. We will put him in the van with Joey and Samm, and she will ride with us. Jeryca, you go on and handle what you got to handle, and we will meet you at the warehouse. Text me when you are finished with what you got to do," Valerie ordered.

"All right, I will see y'all in a little while," Jeryca said.

She kissed Orlando and walked out. She could hear movement coming from inside the house and then she heard the back door open up. She saw shadowy figures moving to and from the different vehicles that were around there.

As she got into her car, she was filled with different emotions. This night would make her or break her, and she hoped that with all the planning she had been doing, everything would work out as she planned.

When she pulled off, she picked up her cell phone. After dialing the number, she placed it on speakerphone. "Hello, Detective Rone please," she said once the operator answered.

She was placed on a brief hold, and then he answered, "Detective Rone speaking."

"Hello, Detective Rone, this is Jeryca Mebane, and I'm ready."

"Are you sure? Once we wire you up and you walk into that warehouse, there is no turning back," Detective Rone replied.

"I'm ready. How long will all this take?" Jeryca asked.

"About two hours or so. Come on in and let's get you hooked up and discuss the details," Detective Rone said.

"All right. See you soon," Jeryca replied.

Chapter Six

Dana woke up and realized she was tied to a chair. She didn't know what was going on, but if Zack was trying to be kinky or was trying to play some kind of game, she wasn't feeling it. She wasn't laughing, but as she thought about it more, she knew that Zack wouldn't play with her like that.

When she looked up, she saw four shadowy figures walking toward her. Her first thought was that it was Chris and Thad. She figured he had somehow found out about Debra and was out for revenge. The shadows became clearer, and she was face-to-face with Orlando, Jeryca, and two other women. She squinted because she knew her eyes had to be playing tricks on her.

Once she realized that it was indeed Jeryca, she asked angrily, "Jeryca, what the fuck are you doing?"

"Do you really have to ask? I'm taking everything from you. You don't deserve to even be breathing right now, Dana. You, Stephanie, and I have allowed your issues to turn other people's lives into chaos. And you two feel no regret," Jeryca replied.

"What the hell are you talking about, Jeryca?" Dana asked.

"I'm talking 'bout the fact that you haven't checked on Travis or Shirley much at all since Farrah's death. I'm talking 'bout all the bodies that are dropping from the bullshit we have been doing, and lastly, I'm talking 'bout you killing Farrah!" Jeryca said angrily.

"What? Jeryca, you have lost your mind," Dana said confusedly.

"Naw, I'm right. You see, I overheard you telling Zack and Brittany about what you had done the night we were all at her house. You went to Shirley's house and held Farrah's son, comforting him, when all along you were the bitch who took his mother from him!" Jeryca shouted.

Dana sat quietly, tears streaming down her face. She searched the room for Zack, but he was nowhere to be found.

Jeryca smiled as she realized who Dana must've been looking for. "Are you looking for Zack? He's down in the car. He sends his regards. Oh, and this is Valerie and Desiree. I met them down in

Florida where we decided that you were a liability and needed to be dealt with. I'm running the show now with Orlando and Zack. Together, we are going to take over the East Coast and make some money. You thought you were the head bitch, but you haven't been for a while. You have been playing right into my hands! I'ma make sure that Farrah gets the perfect headstone, and Travis eats every day. I'm going to make sure that Shirley has the money she needs to take care of him, worry-free. You said you were going to look out for them, but you haven't once reached out to them since the last time we were all there. You are a liar, and you are disloyal," Jeryca sneered.

Valerie and Desiree walked forward and began pouring gasoline around the warehouse. Dana began shouting for Zack to come and help her, but in midscream, Jeryca slapped her. "Bitch, shut the fuck up! You are about to feel the heat of hell in a few moments, something you deserve, Dana, and trust me, Stephanie is next! I loved you and Stephanie. Shit, we all grew up together. How could you let your hate and greed destroy you? Destroy us?" Jeryca cried as she put duct tape across Dana's mouth.

As Valerie lit the match and Desiree poured the last drop of gasoline near the door, Jeryca looked at Dana, who was twisting and turning in her seat. She shook her head and walked out the door, and as she walked away, Valerie dropped the match, and the room lit up with flames.

Jeryca walked out of the warehouse and got into the burgundy Hummer with Orlando, Valerie, and Desiree. When they drove away, she looked in the rearview mirror at Zack and smiled. "It's almost over. We got one more stop to make. You okay, babe?" Jeryca asked Orlando, who was seated in the passenger seat, looking at her sideways.

"Yeah, I just didn't know you had it in you to do that to your homegirl. I'm proud of you. I knew you could be that ride or die chick for me."

Zack sat in the back, listening to Orlando and Jeryca, and he felt somewhat disappointed that he had to turn on Dana as he did. He had to do what he had to do to make the millions that Sergio and Ramon assured him he could make if he followed suit. They had stayed in Florida a few days, and somehow they had taken a liking to Jeryca immediately. He wished that he had gone on and taken Dana with him, because he knew they would've liked her, but it was too late to think about it. Dana was dead, and he had to keep his mind focused on what was important: the money!

Valerie, who was seated next to him, smiled as she placed her hand on his lap. "You can do a whole lot better than Dana anyway."

He laughed. "Oh, yeah? How so?"

"Shit, I can show you when we get to the hotel," she whispered as her hand slid up his thigh to his dick.

He couldn't believe how forward she was, but he would definitely fuck her. His phone started vibrating, and when he looked down at it, he saw a text from Brittany: Is everything good?

He looked at Valerie, smiled, and texted back: Everything is excellent.

He then turned his phone off and laid his head back against the headrest and enjoyed the dick massage that Valerie was giving him.

The group hit the highway, heading to Maryland for a couple of weeks to let the smoke clear. Jeryca felt a calm wash over her that she hadn't felt in months. She was now happy and was finally about to get what she always wanted: a life away from the hood. She could hear the knocking coming from the trunk and Toby screaming. She turned the music up to drown out his cries.

Detectives Rone and Harris rushed toward the warehouse after Jeryca's wire had been disconnected. They were only a few streets over with several other squad cars, waiting for their signal to enter. Once they arrived, they noticed gray clouds of smoke pouring out the windows of the warehouse.

"Officer Craig, you and Thomas secure the back while we secure the front. And get the got-damn fire department out here now!" Detective Rone shouted.

"We're on it, sir!" Officer Craig replied, running full speed around to the back of the building.

"Dammit, Rone, what the fuck do you think happened?" Detective Harris asked as they waited for the fire department to arrive.

"I really don't know, but I don't think we're going to be happy with what we are about to find. That girl ran a scam on us, and we fell for it, man. Maybe I'm too old now for this line of work," Detective Rone said angrily.

The fire trucks and paramedics arrived after a few minutes, and the scene went from wired to chaotic. There were a lot of officers running around, both police and firemen. Curious on-lookers pulled over to see what was going on, and soon there were mobs of people standing around looking.

Once the fire was extinguished, the fire chief escorted Detectives Rone and Harris in. The smell of gasoline was strong, but thankfully, there wasn't a lot of damage to the warehouse. It was mostly the walls and windows that were destroyed.

"Detective Rone! There's something you need to see over here now!" Chief Gillespie yelled.

Detective Rone rushed over, and the ghastly scene that was before him almost caused him to vomit. The smell of burnt flesh filled his nose. "Get the paramedics up here now!" he shouted over to Detective Harris.

Detective Rone bent down on one knee and looked over the body that was still partially bound to a chair. He couldn't make out the face, but there was something familiar about the scene.

As the paramedics arrived, one of them gasped as they assessed the body. "She's still alive! Let's get her stabilized and out of here!"

After they stabilized Dana, they prepared her for transport. The paramedics rushed Dana's burned body out of the warehouse, with Detective Rone close behind. A few reporters had gathered around the perimeter, snapping pictures and shouting questions. Detective Rone knew he would have to answer them, but he wouldn't do it until after they knew what the outcome was going to be with Dana.

Before Detective Rone could give out his orders to the other officers, Fire Chief Andrews halted him in his tracks. "Detective Rone, there's something else inside that you need to see."

"What now?" he whispered to himself. As he walked back into the warehouse, which they had learned belonged to Orlando Graves, he saw a few of his officers taking pictures of what appeared to be a corpse. As he got closer, it was confirmed. The body was burned beyond recognition. The crime scene unit was already collecting forensic evidence from around the area and on the body.

"I hope this isn't the woman we were led here to rescue. Dammit, get the helicopters in the air and dispatch a few units and find Jeryca Mebane!" Detective Rone shouted.

As the officers scattered to do as they were instructed, Detective Rone felt a bit saddened. He didn't know why anyone would torture the two women he had just seen burned in that warehouse. Although the cause of the fire hadn't been officially determined as arson, he knew it was. He knew that Jeryca Mebane was behind it, and he was going to prove it. Whatever was going on, he wasn't going to rest until he put everyone involved behind bars.

"Rone, don't beat yourself up over this. You didn't know that this was going to happen. Let's do our job and find out who did this and put them behind bars," Detective Harris said as he patted Detective Rone on the shoulder.

"I'm two steps ahead of you! Let's finish up here so we can get to the hospital. Call over there and let the hospital staff know that no one is allowed in to see Dana Crisp, period," Detective Rone commanded.

"All right, I will make the call myself. What about the other body that was found?" Detective Harris inquired as the second coroner wheeled the body past them.

"Well, there isn't much we can do there but wait for the forensic pathologist to send us their findings. Make sure they collect as much evidence as they can to identify the body," Rone stated.

"Yes, sir." Detective Harris walked off to talk with the coroner and sign the coroner's paperwork, and make the call to the hospital.

Detective Rone walked back into the warehouse. He didn't know what he was expecting to find, but he was searching for any evidence that could point out the person responsible for the fire and murder. He knew who his culprit was. He just needed evidence. He was going to take Jeryca Mebane down if it was the last thing he did.

After an hour, Detectives Rone and Harris left the warehouse and went straight to the hospital. As soon as they walked in, they were directed to the burn unit on the fourth floor. They were taken to unit 15, where Dana had been stabilized and taken to surgery.

Dr. Schmitz pulled the detectives to the side and whispered, "The next forty-eight hours will be critical for Ms. Crisp. She flatlined once, but we were able to get her back. Her heart is still weak, and we aren't sure if she will pull through this. We had to induce a coma so that the swelling tissue around her face and head can go down. She is on a ventilator, and once the surgery is over, we will make sure that she will rest comfortably. We have our top burn surgeon in with her, and they will remove all the burnt skin and tissue from her face and neck area. She sustained third-degree burns, and most of the scarring is located on the left side of her body. The worst of the damage is up toward her facial area."

"Well, here is my number, and you call me if there are any changes. We will leave a guard outside her door and no one, I repeat, no one is allowed to enter this room without my approval. I don't care if it is Saint Maria! I will stay until the officers arrive and they will alternate rounds," Detective Rone instructed.

"Understood," Dr. Schmitz said.

Once the officers arrived, Detectives Rone and Harris left the hospital and agreed to meet at the hospital the next day. They weren't going to rest until they arrested someone for murder and the heinous crime against Dana Crisp.

Once Detective Rone arrived at the precinct to do his report, he was approached by Officer Jackson. "Sir, may I assist you with this case?"

Detective Rone frowned as he looked at Jackson and asked, "Why do you want to help?"

"I have experience in these types of cases, and I think I can be a great asset to you," she explained.

Officer Jackson was a plump woman in her mid-thirties. She had short hair, and she kept it tied up. She was a natural beauty, and she was good at doing her job. Detective Rone didn't realize that she had experience with arson cases, but he would use any and all resources to solve his case.

"Let me see your credentials, and in the morning, I will talk to Captain Atwater and see if he will let you join us for this case," Rone said tiredly.

"Thank you, sir!" Jackson replied, before walking to her cubby and grabbing her file. She placed it on Rone's desk and walked off.

Detective Rone looked over her file and was extremely impressed with what he was reading. She had over twenty successful drug busts, seven solved murder cases, and nine solved arson cases. She was exactly what he needed for this case and possibly others that he was and would be working on. He was going to see if he could get her promoted to his department.

He typed up his report and clocked out. He knew he wasn't going to get much sleep, but he wanted to take a good shower and relax. He thought about how Dana looked before the fire and after. His heart went out to her more than it should have. He was really taking her assault personally. No one knew how he felt and he couldn't tell anyone, or he'd definitely be released from her case, and he couldn't let that happen.

He was determined to find Jeryca Mebane and whoever else was involved in the attack and attempted murder of Dana Crisp.

Chapter Seven

A year and a half after the tragic fire that Jeryca Mebane and her newfound crew set, Dana Crisp was still recovering from the wounds she had sustained from that fire. She couldn't remember a whole lot about that night, but one image haunted her nightly, and that was Jeryca's evil grin. She was also haunted by the knowledge of her lover Zack's betrayal. Nevertheless, to her surprise, Brittany and Stephanie were there with her every step of the way through her rehabilitation.

After Jeryca attempted to kill Dana, Stephanie was concerned that she was going to be next and decided that the best thing for her to do was move away from the city and out to the country with Dana and Brittany. Jeryca wouldn't be able to find them there. At least, Stephanie hoped she wouldn't. Never in a million years did she ever think that shit would turn out like it had. She was out to do what she had to do to stay alive.

Detective Rone was still working to keep his vow to find and arrest everyone involved in the horrific crime committed against Dana. With his team of detectives, who were as determined as he was to find Jeryca Mebane and her crew, how could they lose?

Thad was struggling to keep his head above water. His life took a drastic turn the day his brother went missing, and soon after, he received a tape in the mail of Toby being beaten to death. He had also learned that Tiffany had been in the same warehouse fire that Dana was found in. He had never felt so angry in his life, and he didn't understand where they went wrong. Thad had no idea that Tim was connected to Sergio and Ramon, but what really didn't register was how they knew it was Toby who killed him. Only one person registered in his mind as a possible snitch, and he was going to get even with that person: the person responsible for his brother's death.

"Okay, Dana, take a deep breath and we will do ten leg lifts. Are you ready?" Roy, her therapist, asked.

"Yeah, I'm ready." Dana sighed. She had suffered severe burns to her face and over 65 percent of her body. Some of her muscles were damaged, which was the reason she couldn't walk. As she sat in her wheelchair, her therapist squatted down and lifted her leg by her calf to the count of ten, during which Dana gave minimal assistance. After an hour with her therapist, Brittany would be there to transport her home.

They had found a nice, secluded area near Poughkeepsie, New York. Brittany closed her practice to help Dana during her time of need, and Stephanie tagged along to help as well. She'd called it quits with Robin after she found her with Chris, and she decided to focus on getting her life on track. With Jeryca being the prime suspect in Tiffany Royster's murder and Dana's attempted murder, Stephanie knew she needed to disappear until they found her. She didn't know why Jeryca did what she did, but as long as she was free, no one was safe.

Stephanie and Brittany had discussed Zack's possible role in everything. Brittany remembered that night. Dana was supposed to meet with him. Zack had called her and told her that he only wanted to meet with Dana, because he wanted to surprise her with a special gift. He explained that the last time he and Dana talked, it ended on a sour note and he knew that Dana wouldn't meet him if he hadn't told her it was about the money.

Brittany couldn't believe she fell for his lie. She had once viewed Zack as a real friend and for him to try to take someone from her who he knew she cared for was unforgivable.

"Hey, *mami,* you ready to go?" Brittany asked as she walked into the therapy room.

"Yes, I am," Dana replied with her head down.

"Don't do that, Dana. What did I tell you? You keep your head up. Don't be ashamed of your scars. You survived something that most haven't. That makes you a strong bitch. Your scars prove that," Brittany lectured her.

Dana smiled, but she knew that her friend was being nice. Her face was hideous, and she wasn't going to pretend it wasn't. Any time Dana was out, she felt the piercing glares from people. Brittany, Stephanie, and Dana's nurse, Rebecca Leary, who was hired by Brittany three weeks after Dana was released from the hospital, would confront anyone they caught staring at Dana. Brittany liked Rebecca right off the bat because, of all the nurses she had interviewed, Rebecca was the only one who didn't cringe at Dana's appearance. All her references checked out and Rebecca seemed to bond with Dana very quickly. Dana, on the other hand, felt useless and that her life was now meaningless. She felt she had no reason to smile anymore.

"How did she do today, Roy?" Brittany asked.

"She did okay. I could feel slight movement in her muscles today when we did our leg lifts. She was really trying to help as much as she could. I know she has an appointment with Dr. Gilmore next week, so I'm going to fax my recommendation for another surgery on her legs," Roy replied.

"Is another surgery necessary?" Dana looked up and asked, annoyed.

"I think it is necessary. Do you want to walk again? This chair isn't becoming on you. It's a prison for you, and I know with the type of surgery I'm suggesting and your willpower, you will walk again. Your muscles were contracting when we were doing your leg lifts today. You need this," Roy answered.

Dana shrugged her shoulders uncaringly and dropped her head again.

Brittany and Rebecca looked at each other with a knowing glance. They both realized that Dana was giving up and they had to help her gain self-confidence somehow.

"Thank you, Roy. We will see you next week," Brittany said as she opened the door for Rebecca, who was wheeling Dana out of the room.

Once they were outside and had Dana comfortably in the car, Rebecca stood at the side of the car, looked at Brittany, and whispered, "She has got to snap out of this funk!"

Brittany agreed with her, and they got into the car and drove away.

Detective Rone was sitting in his office, looking over a case he had been working on for less than a week. He was writing his observation notes when Detective Jackson walked in.

"What's going on, boss? Are we heading out today or what?" she asked.

Detective Rone looked up at his calendar and realized that it was time to go check on Dana. He had been keeping a very close eye on her since the night of the fire. Jeryca had left a cold trail, but he was determined to find her and arrest her for murder, attempted murder, and arson, as well as several other charges.

Since the fire, he had been given a new team of officers of his choosing. Detective Harris couldn't handle being in the homicide department, so he decided to change careers. He was now a parole officer, and he was satisfied. Detective Rone's new lead detective, Emily Jackson, had taken a keen interest in Dana Crisp's case as well. She had been promoted since she started working with Detective Rone a year and a half ago, and she wanted to close the case just as much as he did.

"Yes, we are going."

"Rone, what do you think about Dana's new nurse?" Emily asked.

"She seems like a nice person," Detective Rone answered.

"Yeah, I guess she does," Emily replied, smiling.

"Well, let's head on out and get started. We need to go to Office Depot to see if we can get the surveillance footage for September sixteenth and get a statement from the people who were working that day," Detective Rone stated, referring to his latest case.

"Ten-four!" Emily Jackson said, as she grabbed her folders and walked out the door.

The two exited the building and walked down the steps, greeting other officers as they passed by. It was a cool fall day, and October was right around the corner. As they walked out of the building, Detective Rone inhaled deeply and exhaled. "Fresh air!"

Thad called Chris and asked him to meet him at the trap house, which was the only thing bringing in money for him. After everything that happened between him and Orlando, no one wanted to fuck with Thad on any plays. He really wasn't as focused on getting money as he used to be, because he was still reeling from his brother's death. The vision of how they'd beaten Toby haunted Thad daily. Thad knew that it was a matter of time before they came for him, but he wasn't going to wait around for them to come. He was going to seek out his own revenge on anyone he felt had something to do with Toby's death.

Chris was the one who mostly maintained the trap house. He had brought in some new girls, and the money was flowing constantly, which kept Thad and Chris living comfortably.

When Thad arrived at the trap house, he found Chris in the office looking over the books. "What's up, Chris?" Thad said as he sat down in the chair opposite Chris.

"What's going on, Thad? How are you doing today?" Chris asked.

"Man, just trying to keep my head up. It's hard without Toby," Thad whispered.

Chris knew that Thad was hurting, and even though he still looked at Thad as being a snake, he couldn't turn his back on him at that moment.

"Ay, man, come and ride out with me for a while," Thad said.

"All right. Let me finish this up and I will be ready," Chris said, as he typed in some numbers on the calculator.

Thad looked around the room and memories of Toby flooded his mind. He shook his head several times and finally excused himself. "Ay, man, I'ma wait for you in the car."

"I'm right behind you, bro!" Chris replied.

Five minutes later, Chris was in the car heading down the highway with Thad. Thad was smoking on a blunt and was strangely quiet. Chris looked at him and quickly looked out the window. He wondered where Thad was going and finally asked, "Ay, man, where we going?"

"I figured we'd go see an old friend. It's way overdue, if you ask me," Thad said emotionlessly, which instantly put Chris on edge.

Chris again glanced out the window and suddenly recognized a few buildings, which set him more on edge. He didn't know what was going through Thad's mind, but he wasn't going out like a sucker if Thad tried him. Chris put his hand to his side, because if he had to get to his gun that was on his hip, he would be able to pull it out quickly.

Thad finally pulled into Austin's car garage, which looked deserted and dark. After Thad parked the car, he looked over at Chris. "Come on, nigga, get out!"

Chris rolled his eyes slightly, exhaled hard, and exited the car. As the two men entered the garage, they spotted Austin lying under a car, changing what appeared to be brakes.

"Hey, now! What's up, Austin?" Thad said as he approached the car.

Chris lingered close to the door of the garage, keeping a small distance between him and Thad. Austin slid away from under the car, stood up, gave Thad a brotherly hug, and replied, "Damn, man, it's been a while. What you been up to?"

"Shit, nothing at all," Thad answered. "Just been trying to keep my head above water, you know. You've been MIA yourself, dude."

"I know, man. I had to make a few changes with my life. My girl got pregnant, and I couldn't continue on the path I was on. I had to think about the future of my baby. So I told Toby I couldn't fuck around like that. He said he understood. What's up, Chris? You standing over there and ain't said shit," Austin said, looking at Chris.

"I'm just paying attention to my surroundings, that's all. You know how that is," Chris said calmly.

Thad rubbed his face a few times, looking very serious. "So you saying you spoke to Toby?"

"Uh, yeah, man. I told him that I couldn't—"

Thad interrupted Austin. "Yeah, I heard that, but when did you speak to him is my question," Thad continued to pry.

"A few months back! Yeah, it was very brief," Austin replied.

"Man, Chris, come on over here with us. You're standing over there like you scared of something. Did you just hear what Austin said?" Thad asked, with a look on his face that Chris couldn't quite read.

"I feel you on that. I haven't heard from Toby in a few months, though. What the hell he been up to?" Austin asked as he reached to grab a lug wrench and placed it down on the mat he had been lying on.

No one but Thad and Chris knew that Toby had been killed. They were told that if they went to the cops, they would be next. Thad knew his time was coming anyway, so he planned to get a little vengeance himself. When Austin asked about Toby, it set something off inside Thad. He stood and watched as Austin lay back down on the mat, slid back under the car, and continued to work on the brakes. Chris shook his head and walked slowly over to where Thad was standing.

"Chris, Austin wants to know what's up with Toby. Why don't you tell him?"

Chris looked at Thad with a frown on his face. "Are you serious?"

"Hell yeah! Tell the man!" Thad growled.

"Well uh, Austin, man, Toby was killed a little over a year ago, and we were told not to tell anyone or else we would be next," Chris mumbled.

A loud thud was heard from under the car as Austin dropped the wrench he was holding. "Say what?" he asked quietly.

"You heard him! As if you didn't know! There ain't no damn way you fucking talked to Toby!" Thad said through clenched teeth.

Before Austin could move or respond, Thad kicked away the jack that had the car hoisted up, and the car fell, crashing down on top of Austin and crushing his ribs.

"What the fuck!" Chris shouted as he jumped back. He had no idea that Thad was planning on doing that.

Thad bent down and looked under the car. Blood was seeping out from under it, and Austin could be heard gasping for air. "Bitch, I know you had something to do with my brother getting murdered. What, did you think that you were going to take over our business? Bitch, you were never going to be us! Yeah, it took me a minute to figure it out, but you were the link to Sergio and Ramon. I know you were. You fucking got my brother killed, you snitch!"

"I didn't do it!" Austin whispered as his life slowly slipped away.

Thad stood up and looked at Chris. "Let's get out of here."

The two left Austin's shop and headed back to the trap house. Chris looked over at Thad. "What if he didn't do it?"

"That muthafucka had something to do with it. Why the hell would he lie about talking to Toby?" Thad yelled.

"Man, I don't know. I'm just saying what if he didn't have anything to do with it. You just killed a man without any proof that he did anything."

"I know the bastard was the snitch, but shit, if he wasn't the snitch then I may need to place my focus elsewhere, huh?" Thad said, glancing over at Chris.

"I know you aren't looking at me like I'm the one who had bruh hemmed up! I ain't had shit to do with anything!" Chris replied.

"Mm-hmm. I hope not! Shit could get real crazy, if you know what I mean," Thad mumbled as he turned the music up and continued to drive, not uttering another word.

Chris now felt threatened, and he decided he had to figure out a way to get Thad before Thad got him.

Chapter Eight

Pam Mebane woke up Thursday morning and lay in bed, hoping that she would hear from Jeryca. They were out of school for a teachers' workday, and Pam didn't know what she was going to do. She got up, took her shower, and dried off. As she opened the door, she heard her mother talking to Todd. Their voices were slightly raised, and Pam slowly shut the door so she could eavesdrop without being seen.

"Damn, all I'm asking is that you call her and see if she will loan you a few thousand dollars! It's not like she ain't got it, Sheila! You told me yourself that Jeryca sends you money every week to help out with Pam. All I'm asking you to do is ask her for a few thousand dollars. You don't understand. These guys are going to kill me if I don't come up with their money!" she heard Todd yell.

"I don't want to ask my daughter for that much money! What am I supposed to tell her I need it for?" she heard her mother ask.

"Baby, please, I don't have anyone else to ask! Do you want to see me dead?" he asked Sheila.

There was a brief silence, and then Pam heard her mother sigh. "No, I don't want to see you dead. I will see what I can do. I just got to come up with a good excuse for needing the money."

"Thanks, baby. You are the best," Todd said, before opening up the door to Sheila's bedroom.

Pam quietly and quickly closed the bathroom door all the way and locked it. She couldn't believe how gullible her mother was. Jeryca was right about her, and the more she saw her mother interact with Todd, the more Pam resented her.

After Todd left, Pam walked out of the bathroom and into the kitchen where her mother was fixing some coffee. "What's for breakfast?"

"No 'good morning'?" her mother asked.

"Excuse me. Good morning, Mom. Are you cooking breakfast?"

"You are old enough to cook for yourself. I'm not your servant!" she answered agitatedly.

This took Pam by surprise, because she had never heard such venom in her mother's voice before. At least, not toward her.

"Neva mind, Ma! I will just go hungry!" Pam said, shaking her head.

"I know you will if you waiting for me to cook something. Y'all grown asses around here kill me expecting somebody to wait on you hand and foot. I'm not gonna do it," Sheila slurred.

Pam looked at her mom, wondering why she was talking like that. As she walked closer to her, she realized that her mother had been drinking, which was out of character for her. Pam walked out the door and immediately dialed her sister's number, but she got no answer.

Pam left for a few hours to get away from her mother, but when she returned, a sickening sight greeted her. Her mother was on her knees, giving Todd a massive head job. They were so engrossed in each other they didn't see or hear her come in. She immediately turned around and ran from the house. She felt sick to her stomach. She could barely tolerate hearing them having sex, but to witness firsthand her mom giving him head was too much for her. She didn't understand why they would even be having sex in the living room. They were well aware that she was going to come back home.

She walked to the park, sat on the bench, and tried Jeryca again, but again got no answer. After about an hour, Pam noticed that there was an older gentleman sitting across from her, just staring at her. She looked around and was slightly at ease seeing that there were other people sitting around. She walked over and began talking with a few kids she knew from school. She glanced back to where the man had been, and he was gone.

She decided to call her mom to let her know she was on her way home. She didn't want to walk in on any more of her mother and Todd's sickening exploits. After she got off the phone with her mother, she waited around until the other kids left and she followed suit. She wasn't going to walk home alone. It wasn't the first time she had seen that weird man lurking around.

When Pam walked into the house, her mom was in the kitchen cooking. She walked past Todd without even acknowledging his existence.

"Ay, girl, don't you know how to speak when you walk into the house? I know your mammy taught you better than that!" Todd sneered.

Pam ignored his question and went straight to her room. She could hear Todd telling her mother that she needed to teach her how to respect others or he would.

Pam rushed into the living room where Todd was, and she stood directly in his face. "Nigga, you ever think you gon' do something to me, it will be the last time you think about doing something! I will make sure you regret it! I'm not scared of yo' punk ass, you bum! Get a job with your lazy-ass self! Stop trying to get my mother to take money from my sister to pay your debts, bitch!"

Sheila ran into the living room and pushed her way in between Pam and Todd. "Pam, go in your room! Now, he is a guest, and you will be respectful. Do you hear me?"

Pam looked at her mother in disbelief. She couldn't believe that her mother was actually taking Todd's side. She looked at Todd and saw that he was smirking and nodding. Pam rushed to her room and dialed Jeryca's number again. She still didn't get an answer, so she left her a message.

"Hey, sis, please call me as soon as possible. This muthafucka just lost his mind insinuating that he is going to do something to me, and Mom has lost hers as well taking up for him. Please call me as soon as you can. Oh, and, sis, I think someone is following me. I don't know who he is, but I've seen him a few times. Please call me back, okay?" Pam hung up and lay across her bed until she fell asleep.

Pam left her house early the next morning, heading to school. She usually wouldn't have left that early, but she didn't want any more run-ins with her mom. She knew that Todd had already left for work two hours before she walked out of the house, because she ran into him as he walked half naked into the bathroom. She needed to get away from her mother's house quickly, and she prayed that Jeryca would send for her soon, just as she'd promised. She dialed Jeryca's number once again, praying she answered.

Miami, Florida

"J, baby, you got a phone call!" Orlando yelled.

"Who is it?" Jeryca asked.

"It's Pam. She wants to talk to you," Orlando answered.

"Bring the phone to me please, sir," Jeryca yelled.

Orlando took the phone to Jeryca and then answered his cell phone, which had been ringing off and on all morning. Orlando knew who it was, but he was trying to hold off from talking to them, at least until he could make up a lie that would work. As he walked away to talk business, Jeryca was cleaning herself up so she could talk to her sister.

"What's up, baby girl?" she asked as she walked into the bedroom.

"Jeryca, Momma is tripping. She don't talk to me like she used to, we argue all the time, and she lets her boyfriend say whatever he wants to me! Our relationship has worsened, and it's driving me crazy."

"Shit, you know how Momma is. You just got to deal with it, sis," Jeryca replied.

"I just can't. And this lame-ass boyfriend thinks the sun rises and sets on him. Momma be so far up his ass, she does everything he tells her to, and, sis, she has started drinking. I know it's all because of him. I swear, I can't stand him," Pam said.

"He can't be that bad, sis. Give him a break. He might be cool if you just relax on him," Jeryca pointed out.

"Jeryca, you just don't know. I'm telling you something isn't right with this man and Momma ain't trying to see it. He looks at me in a way that makes me feel uncomfortable, sis!" Pam cried.

"Well, I am still gonna send for you just as soon as I can talk to Mom, which I know will make you feel better," Jeryca replied, understanding Pam a lot more than she wanted to confess.

"Please make that happen. Oh, and he asked Mom to ask you for some money so he can pay some type of money he owe out," Pam squealed.

"He what? I know that nigga don't think I'ma send any money to him for anything!" Jeryca laughed.

"Don't tell Mom I told you that 'cause she supposed to be asking you soon and using me as a reason for needing the money. They don't even know that I know anything about it. I overheard his beggin' ass pleading with Mom while I was in the bathroom," Pam explained.

"Shit, I'm glad you told me that. I can't believe that nigga and Mom think they can trick me out of some cash. After all I do for Mom, she would really do that?" Jeryca asked.

"I told you, she isn't herself, Jeryca. He has her brainwashed," Pam said.

"More like dick whipped!" Jeryca corrected her, laughing.

Pam laughed. "I love you, sis!"

"I love you too. I will call Mom tomorrow and talk to her about you coming here, okay?" Jeryca replied.

"Okay. Talk to you later, sis!" Pam said.

After she concluded her call with Pam, she went searching for Orlando. They had bought a two-story, four-bedroom condo close to the beach. Jeryca was living the life she always knew she was destined to live. Orlando had become Sergio's top man in Florida, and he moved shipments all up and down the East Coast, as well as in Hawaii. They had their own personal yacht and drove around on the streets in a black Mercedes-Benz SUV and a pearl white and pink Cadillac Escalade. Jeryca was living the life of a queen, and she wasn't going to give it up for anyone.

She maintained contact with Valerie and Desiree almost daily. They had become friends and executed three plays together, from which Jeryca's cut was a total of $400,000. She sent money home to her mother regularly, and her mother appreciated every dime. But what she really wanted was for Jeryca to move back home where she belonged. Jeryca refused, knowing that the police were probably looking for her. She and Orlando had been given new identities with Ramon's help and were known to the locals there as Betty and Vick Logan.

Jeryca had to take the good with the bad, and her current way of life was worth a few changes. She had heard that Dana survived the fire but was dealing with serious injuries due to it. Jeryca wasn't completely satisfied with that, but there was little that she could do about it.

When she found Orlando, he was sitting at the bar with his head bent. "Baby, what's going on?" she asked.

"We got to find a way to get Sergio and Ramon some of the money that we owe them. They aren't going to keep waiting for us to pay them. We knew what we had to do when we decided to take on this job, and we aren't holding up our end of the bargain. They have been very lenient with us," he explained.

"But we been putting in the work to get that money, not them! I don't understand how they figure it's cool that we get thirty percent of the money we make! That shit isn't right at all, and I know I'm not the only one who feels like that. I didn't think you were the kind of man who would let another muthafucka dictate how you move," Jeryca said angrily.

"Look, Jeryca, I'm not gonna have this conversation with you anymore. Stop spending all the gotdamn money like you are. I'm not playing with your ass!" Orlando said angrily. He stormed out of the condo, leaving Jeryca staring at the door, fuming.

Jeryca stomped to the bedroom and threw herself down. As she lay there, her mind drifted back to the conversation she and Pam had just had. Jeryca closed her eyes and sighed as the past flooded her thoughts.

When Jeryca was nine, her mother began dating a new guy, and she moved him in after only knowing him for a few weeks. His name was Greg, and his first night in the house he started making comments that made her feel very uncomfortable. She was certain that her mother had heard a few of them and yet said nothing.

One day, Sheila left her at home alone with Greg, and he began making very degrading comments, calling her a whore and saying that she wouldn't ever be good for anything just like her worthless mother. He told her that Sheila didn't love her and she was a thorn in her mother's side. He assured her that if he killed her, her mother wouldn't care at all. Jeryca cringed at what he said and believed it to be true. After all, her mother had started acted extremely differently toward her once Greg had moved in.

The comments soon led to fondling and then, one fateful day, Greg raped Jeryca! She was only nine years old at the time, and when he told her that he would kill her and her mother if she told on him, she believed him. He raped her twice more, and after the second time, she ran away from home.

She went and stayed with Farrah and her mom. She explained to Shirley what was going on and that she would die if she had to go back. She also begged Shirley not to call the police, because she was too embarrassed to face anyone. Shirley agreed not to call the police, but the following day she contacted Sheila and told her what Jeryca had shared with her.

Sheila didn't believe her at first and fussed at Jeryca for spreading lies. She told her that she was going to have her picked up for being a runaway if she didn't come home immediately. Jeryca remembered that she had never felt so hurt in her life.

A few weeks later, after Jeryca returned home, Greg attempted to rape Jeryca once again, but she fought him hard. He had her on the bed, and after being bitten and scratched one time too many, Greg hauled off and slapped Jeryca across the face. He had gotten her pants down halfway when, all of a sudden, Greg screamed out in pain. Sheila had walked in, caught him in the act, and bashed him across his lower back with the broom handle. She hit him repeatedly until he fell to the floor, screaming and squirming in pain. Jeryca jumped up and ran out of the room, while her mother continued to beat Greg with the broom, yelling and screaming for him to get out of her house and never to return. She vowed that she would kill him if he ever came within a hundred feet of her or Jeryca again.

After Greg left, Sheila went to look for Jeryca, who was in the bathroom sitting on the floor, crying and shaking. Her face was red where Greg had slapped her. Sheila grabbed a towel, wet it with cold water, and pressed it against Jeryca's face. She had looked her daughter in the face, uttering, "I'm sorry I didn't listen to you, but, sweetie, you got to promise me that you won't utter one word of this to anyone. I don't want or need anybody in my business. You will be okay. I'm going to make sure of that."

Jeryca had sat speechless on the floor and vowed that she was going to escape the hood at any cost, and never be anything like her mom. That day, little Jeryca had no other choice but to grow up.

Jeryca quickly snapped out of her thoughts as her cell phone began to ring. She grabbed it off the nightstand. "Hello?" she answered.

"Hey, boo, what are you doing?" Valerie asked.

"Nothing right now. What you up to, sis?" she asked.

"Just got off the plane. Waiting on Zack to pick me up."

"Oh, okay! That's what's up. I'm glad you made it there safely. How long you been waiting for Zack?" Jeryca asked.

"We just landed. We got in a little earlier than we were supposed to. Girl, I'm so ready to see this nigga! I missed him so much," Valerie said, sounding anxious.

"You really like him, huh?" Jeryca asked.

"Girl, yes! He makes me feel like no other man has ever made me feel before." Valerie laughed.

"Well, I'm glad y'all are getting it together, chick, but I'm gonna let you go 'cause I got a million and one things on my mind, and I need to get myself together," Jeryca explained.

"Okay, I was just letting you know I made it safe. You get you some rest. You sound tired," Valerie replied.

"I'ma try. Talk to you later," Jeryca said, before hanging up and lying back on the bed. "I won't let anyone hurt my sister like they hurt me. I will die on that!" Jeryca whispered to herself.

Tennessee

Zack walked into Sal's and ordered a sub. He had just left the gym and was heading home to shower before he drove to the airport to pick Valerie up. He was enjoying his new life, but he missed Dana a lot. He hated that he had to turn on Dana as he did, but the amount of money he made and continued to make dealing with Orlando and Jeryca was worth the loss. He heard through mutual acquaintances that Dana survived the fire and was confined to a wheelchair. It pained him to hear that. In his opinion, Dana would have been better off dead. She shouldn't have to suffer as they'd told him she was.

"That will be six bucks even, sir," the cashier told him, interrupting his thoughts.

"All right, thanks." As he turned to walk away, his cell phone started ringing. "Hey, baby! What's up?" he asked.

"We got in early, daddy, and I'm waiting here at the airport for you, and I can't wait to see you," Valerie cooed.

"Damn, bae, I just left the gym, and I haven't even gotten the chance to take a shower yet," he replied.

"Well, that's cool. I like you musty, and besides, we can take a shower together when we get to your place," Valerie said.

"All right, I'm on my way then. I can't wait to see you either," he said before hanging up.

Zack arrived at the airport twenty minutes later and spotted Valerie right away. He really liked her, but he just couldn't get Dana off his mind. He tried to shake the thought of her out of his head, but all the way to the airport, his mind had been on Dana.

"Hey, baby. I'm glad to see you also. Come on, let's get out of here," he said as he grabbed her luggage.

"Damn, no kiss for me? Humph. You couldn't have missed me that much," Valerie said, pouting.

"Come here, momma, and let me taste those lips. You know I missed your ass. I just got a lot on my mind," Zack said as he dropped the luggage and reached out for Valerie.

"That's more like it!" Valerie said, before locking into a passionate kiss with Zack.

Zack pulled back, grabbed her luggage, and proceeded to the car. Valerie stood there, watching Zack for a second, before following him to the car.

Zack turned around. "Come on, Dana, with your slow ass."

Valerie stopped in her footsteps and glared at Zack.

"What's wrong with you?" he asked, once he realized she was watching him.

Valerie put on her most glamorous fake smile. "Nothing. Just watching you walk," she lied, thinking, *he doesn't realize that he just called me Dana*. She wanted to go off, but she didn't want to ruin her weekend before it got started. However, she was going to find a way to hurt him as he had just hurt her.

As Zack pulled off, he prayed that Valerie hadn't heard him mistakenly call her Dana. He knew that Valerie wouldn't like that at all. The two rode down the expressway, each in their own thoughts.

Valerie glanced over at him once more and smiled. *Yes, bittersweet get back!*

Chapter Nine

It had been over a year since Travis had lost his mother and father. Farrah was his everything, and Travis was still having a rough time accepting that she was gone. He knew what death was, but he didn't understand why his parents were taken from him. His grandmother, Shirley, tried her best to make him understand, but she didn't understand herself. Farrah was perfect in her eyes, and she never imagined that she'd be taken from her in such a manner, nor did she imagine that she would be left to take care of a young boy Travis's age.

Travis often asked about his father, and each time, Shirley managed to speak kind words of him, even though she felt he had gotten what he deserved in prison. The three guys responsible for his death were all charged with his murder and were awaiting trial. They told her that the man who actually killed Larry was already facing two other murder charges and would probably face the death penalty.

Jeryca had kept in touch as she promised and sent money, as well as gifts for Travis throughout the year, but Dana and Stephanie had disappeared. She called them repeatedly but got no answer. She knew that Dana was dealing with a lot, but in Shirley's opinion, Dana still could've called from time to time to check on Travis. He loved those girls, and she felt it was wrong for them to forget about him after all they had shared with Farrah.

"Grandma! Grandma! Look what I found!" Travis shouted as he ran and hopped on Shirley's lap.

"Travis, you can't jump on Grandma like that. You know my bones are frail. But what did you find?" she asked.

"I found this picture of Mommy and Daddy in my toy box. Look!" he exclaimed.

Shirley looked at the picture, and Farrah looked happy. "She looks just like her dad," she whispered.

"Grandma, what did my mommy's dad look like?" Travis asked.

"Here, come with me to my room," Shirley said as she stood up.

She walked to her closet, took down an old hat box, and sat on her bed. "Come and sit next to me," she said as she patted the bed.

Travis sat down next to his grandma as she opened the box and rummaged through hundreds of pictures until she found one of Farrah's father.

She handed the picture to Travis. "This is your grandfather. His name is Nygen Lee. He lives in China, which is his homeland. I met him two years before your mother was born. His family wasn't too happy about me and him seeing each other, so after finding out I was pregnant they forced him to give us up, threatening to disown him. He has only seen your mother twice, and I haven't spoken to him in a long, long time," she told him.

"Grandma, what's 'disown'?" Travis asked.

"Well, baby, they were basically going to throw him out of the family," she explained.

"Oh. They can't do that, can they?" he asked.

"Yes, they can do whatever they want, baby. That's how some grownups act when their loved one does something they don't like," she said.

"That's mean, Grandma. Did he like my mommy when he saw her?" Travis asked.

"Baby, when you can understand more we will talk more about this, okay? Just know that, because of how your mother's father treated her, that's the reason she fought so hard to keep your father in your life."

Travis laid his head on her arm and began to cry. "I miss Mommy and Daddy, Grandma. I wish they were here."

Shirley hugged her grandson and rocked him as he cried. Travis had been very strong following both his parents' deaths and only had a few breakdowns. Shirley tried not to cry, but as Travis's tears flowed, so did hers.

That afternoon, after Shirley put Travis to bed for his nap, she decided she was going to attempt to contact Dana and Stephanie once more and see if they could drop by and see Travis. After all, he was their godson.

Dana left therapy Thursday afternoon tired and somewhat withdrawn. She never imagined that recovery would be so difficult. Stephanie had driven her, because Brittany had to take care of a few things. Brittany had been missing in action lately, which made Dana nervous. It was hard for her to trust anyone anymore. She felt that karma was paying her back for all the awful things she had done. She had told Brittany once that if she had to do it all over again, she would. Brittany had laughed, but Dana was serious. Even if karma kept at her, she didn't regret anything she had done.

Once Rebecca and Stephanie had Dana secured in the car, Rebecca told the two ladies to wait for her. She had to run back in and get her cell phone. She explained that she thought she left it in the bathroom.

Dana frowned and looked over at Stephanie. "Didn't she have her cell phone in her hand before she helped put me in the car?"

"I don't know. I wasn't paying too much attention, but why would she have to lie about leaving her phone inside the center if she didn't? Don't make sense to me," Stephanie said.

"I don't know why people do a lot of the things they do, but they do them. I don't know, Steph. Something about this just doesn't sit right with me," Dana replied.

"Dana, you are just being paranoid thinking that someone isn't trustworthy. Has she ever treated you in a manner where you felt she wanted to harm you?" Stephanie asked.

"Well, no, but—"

"But nothing, Dana. Give her a chance, okay? Please. Do it for me."

Dana groaned and nodded in agreement when her cell phone started ringing. "Hello," she answered.

"Hey, Dana, this is Shirley. How are you doing?"

"I'm good, Miss Shirley, and you? How is T Man doing?" Dana asked, glancing over at Stephanie, who was watching Dana with her eyes wide.

"I'm doing okay. It's still hard without my Farrah here, but with God on my side, I can't go wrong. My reason for calling you is that Travis has been asking about you girls. I was hoping you and Stephanie could stop by and pay him a visit one day."

"I'd love that. I miss little T Man. When can we stop by?" Dana asked.

"Dana, we don't really go anywhere, so anytime is good. You just let me know when you are coming," Shirley replied.

"Well, we can come tomorrow. I'm just now leaving my appointment, and I'm really tired, so I need to get some rest," Dana said.

"Sounds good. I hope I'm not being rude, dear, but how is your recovery going, sweetie?" Shirley asked.

Dana stalled a bit before answering. "It's going okay, just taking more time than I'd like to get back to my old self." Dana felt rather weird about Shirley inquiring about her health, knowing she was responsible for her daughter losing her life.

Stephanie waited until Dana got off the phone. "Okay, Miss Daisy, where to next?"

Dana looked at Stephanie and broke out in laughter. Stephanie was the only person who could make such a joke and get away with it. "Shirley wants us to come and see Travis. She said he has been asking for us. Are you up to going?"

"Anything to keep you out of that closet space you call a room," Stephanie replied.

Dana didn't respond. She looked out the window and hummed to "Birthday Suit" by The Weeknd. She used music to tune people out when they weren't saying anything that she was interested in hearing.

A few minutes later, Rebecca walked out of the center, smiling and waving her phone at the two women. Stephanie looked over at Dana. "I told you, you were paranoid for nothing."

Dana didn't say a word as Rebecca got into the car.

"I thought I was going to have to tear that place apart looking for my phone, but thankfully someone found it in the bathroom and left it at the front desk. It's a wonderful thing that we still have people who are honest."

Dana rolled her eyes and glanced over at Stephanie with a funny look.

"Oh! Let's go to the mall and pick up a few things for Travis. You want to do that?" Stephanie asked, breaking the awkward silence.

Dana looked at Stephanie as if she had grown two heads. "You know I'm not going to no mall. Look at me. I'm not dressed for that."

"It's just the mall, Dana. Come on. Let's hang out for a while. We hardly do anything," Stephanie replied.

Dana sighed and shook her head, but she agreed to go. They arrived at the mall, and once Stephanie and Rebecca got Dana comfortably out of the car and into her chair, they headed into the mall. Rebecca excused herself, letting Dana and Stephanie know that she had to use the restroom, but she would find them when she finished.

Dana and Stephanie went from one store to another, picking out shoes, clothes, and a few toys for Travis. As they were heading out of Toys "R" Us, they bumped into Chris, and Dana's heart dropped. She didn't know what was going to happen. She knew that they didn't have anything to do with the fire, but she wondered if they knew that she and the girls were responsible for the robbery, because it was strange to see Chris so far away from the city.

Chris smiled as he approached the ladies. "Hello. I haven't seen you ladies in a while. How are you two doing? And who was that lovely lady who came in with y'all?" he asked.

"We are doing just fine, and that was Dana's nurse Rebecca. How are you doing?" Stephanie replied nonchalantly.

"I've been good, been holding down the fort. You know how I do. Dana, I am so sorry about what happened to you. You look good, though," Chris said, looking Dana over.

"Thank you," Dana replied, rolling her eyes.

"Um, Stephanie, can I speak to you for a second?" he asked.

Stephanie looked at Dana and back to Chris. "I can't leave Dana here by herself."

"It won't take but a second. Just walk with me to the Locker Room. You ain't even got to go all the way. Please," he begged.

"Go ahead, Stephanie, I will be okay," Dana said, seeing the urgency not only in Chris's eyes, but also in Stephanie's eyes.

"I'll just be a second," Stephanie whispered.

The couple walked away, and Dana watched them intently. She hoped Stephanie wouldn't fall for Chris's lies. After a few seconds, she saw Stephanie take out her phone and look over to her. Dana turned her head quickly, not wanting Stephanie to see her staring at them. Suddenly Rebecca appeared around the corner, smiling as she hung up the phone. Dana envied Rebecca and Stephanie because they seemingly had people who were interested in them and she had no one.

"Hey, doll, what's going on inside that lovely brain of yours?" she asked. She stood behind Dana and pushed her to the water fountain and sat down on the bench next to it.

"Just tired, that's all," Dana answered.

A few minutes later, Stephanie was walking back toward them. She didn't say a word as she pushed Dana out of the mall.

Austin's family had held a private funeral with only his family and closest friends right after his death, and then they had him cremated. They decided, after receiving several inquiries weeks later, to do a dedication of his life, where anyone who wanted to show their respect could. They had placed an announcement in the local newspaper, detailing the memorial.

After mulling over the idea for a few days, Thad decided he was going to attend. He needed to get closure on Toby's death, and he felt that was a great way to get it. He was going to get Chris to go with him, whether he wanted to or not. He called Chris but didn't get an answer. "Hey, this is Thad. When you pick me up tomorrow, I want to run something by you. I hope you will be on time, too, man. Get at me when you get this message."

Thad hung up the phone and lay across the bed. He was filled with so many emotions he didn't know which way to turn. He didn't know who he could trust. He thought about Chris's behavior and felt really funny about it. If he had to take him out as well, he would. He wasn't going to leave anything to chance. He knew his life was going to be short-lived, so he was going to take out as many traitors as he could. Revenge would be bittersweet.

After an hour, Thad's phone started ringing. Looking at the caller ID and seeing Private on it, he already knew who it was. He wasn't going to answer it. It was that time of the month again when Ramon and Sergio reminded him that they hadn't forgotten him.

He threw his cell phone against the wall, and it crashed and broke in pieces. He lay back and threw his arm across his face and slipped into an unconscious state.

The next day, Stephanie, Brittany, and Dana drove to Brooklyn to see Travis. Rebecca had requested the day off, so she didn't accompany them on the trip. It took about two hours for them to get to Shirley's, so when they arrived, Dana was in need of a bathroom break. When they walked in, Travis rushed Stephanie, hugging her tightly around her waist. She squatted down and talked to Travis, while Brittany wheeled Dana to the bathroom.

Once she was in the bathroom, Travis whispered, "What's wrong with Aunt Dana?"

"She was in a bad accident, sweetie, but she is the same Auntie Dana and you ain't got to be afraid to talk to her, touch her, or kiss her," Stephanie answered.

Just then, there was a knock at the door, and a few seconds later, Thad and Chris were walking through the door at the same time Dana was being wheeled out of the bathroom. Her expression spoke volumes as she looked into the eyes of Thad Royster.

Before she could react, Travis ran over and grabbed her hand. "I love you, Auntie Dana. I'm glad you are all right."

Dana felt tears gather up in her eyes as Travis crawled up in her lap and kissed her on her cheek. She felt a pang of guilt as Farrah's family embraced her with all her current ailments. She hugged Travis and talked to him for a few minutes before she realized that Stephanie was outside talking to Chris. Had she planned to have him meet them there, knowing it would make her feel awkward? A thousand questions ran through her mind.

"Auntie Dana, you want to see my new truck?" Travis asked.

"Uh, yes, I would. Where is it?" Dana asked.

"It's in my room. Would you like to see it too, Uncle Thad?" he asked.

"Yes, I would, thank you," Thad replied.

As the trio disappeared into Travis's room, with Thad pushing Dana in, Brittany sat back and prayed that Dana kept her composure with Thad. She knew that Dana had some unresolved feelings toward him and his friends.

After a few minutes, Travis came running out of his room and Brittany immediately assumed that something was wrong, until he ran up to his grandma and asked her where the photo album was.

"Auntie Dana and Uncle Thad want to see the pictures we took when we went to Disneyland," he said excitedly.

"Let me see if I can find it," she replied, laughing.

After she located the photo album and gave it to Travis, he skipped off singing. She looked at Brittany and smiled. "I haven't seen him this happy in a long time. It's a wonderful thing seeing Dana and Thad in the same room together. I know the girls blamed the guys for what Larry did, and to tell you the truth, I did also for a while, until they showed up on my doorstep and we discussed everything. I realized that they had nothing to do with what Larry did to my sweet Farrah. I miss her so much, you know. There isn't a day that passes that I don't think of her. I see her in Travis in so many ways. When he smiles, when he cries, when he sleeps; she is all around here."

Brittany had tears welling up in her eyes as she listened to Shirley talk about her daughter. Shirley was also in tears as she talked, but her smile never faltered.

After about fifteen minutes, Dana and Thad emerged from Travis's room, laughing and playing with Travis, who was sitting on Dana's lap as Thad pushed them into the living room.

They left about an hour later, and as they drove off, Dana looked in the rearview mirror at Stephanie. "So did you and Chris have a nice chat?"

"Yes, we did. It was refreshing to talk to him without arguing. I think we're growing up," Stephanie replied laughing.

"Um-hmm. Well, I guess that's why you were so eager to come today," Dana implied sarcastically.

Stephanie laughed. "What you mean by that, Dana?"

"I'm saying, when y'all were talking at the mall I'm sure you told him we were coming here and made plans to meet him here," Dana said.

"Ain't nobody planned to meet Chris anywhere! What the fuck are you talking about, Dana?" Stephanie groaned.

"Again, I'm talking about how you ran into this man just yesterday, and today he conveniently shows up at Shirley's house while we were there. That shit was planned and you know it! I guess you turning out to be a snake just like—" Dana started, but was cut off by Brittany.

"Ay, Dana, chill out! Why are you trying to start something? That girl ain't set nothing up. You tripping!"

"Bitch, who the fuck do you think you checking? I knew y'all two were against me, and it's showing daily. It wouldn't shock me if both of y'all had something to do with Thad and Chris showing up there," Dana cried.

Stephanie laughed again and stared out the window. She was grinding her teeth to keep from cussing Dana out. She also wondered who Dana was about to call a traitor. Something wasn't right, and she was going to find out what if it killed her. She didn't know how much more she could handle before she really snapped, pushed Dana's ass into a pond somewhere, and watched her crippled ass try to swim. Stephanie laughed at the image that formed in her mind.

"Dana, you are paranoid for real. We aren't doing anything but trying to help you. You are just like a sister to us, and we got your best interest at heart. Stop thinking everyone is against you," Brittany said.

"Whatever. No one really has my back. I know y'all feel like you're obligated to help me, but on the real, I'd rather be in a rehabilitation center getting 'round-the-clock care. That way, you can live your life without having to worry about me," Dana replied sadly.

"Girl, if you don't shut the fuck up . . . Even if you weren't living with me, I'd still worry about your ass. Stop acting like a big kid. Yes, you are stuck in that wheelchair, but God willing, you will walk again. You can't just give up hope. And I'm here for the long haul so, again, stop talking that crazy-ass nonsense," Brittany scolded her.

Dana dropped her head and started to cry, not because of the sincerity in Brittany's voice, but because she was angry and couldn't do anything about it. She was confined to where she sat and couldn't get out of that spot until somebody helped her. She wished she could hop out of the car at the stoplight and go her separate way and head as far away as possible from Brittany and that traitor, Stephanie, but she couldn't. When she got back to the house, she was going to make a few calls and go off on her own, without either of the two women currently in her presence.

Chapter Ten

Chris and Thad left Shirley's house a short time after Dana and Stephanie left. Thad too had questions for Chris. "So what did you and Stephanie talk about?"

"Shit, man, we just talked about old times. I tell you, I do miss her a lot. If I had just followed my heart when I was with her, I wouldn't be without her now," Chris answered.

Thad looked at Chris for a few seconds and laughed. "Nigga, don't tell me your ass is whooped! You pussy whipped, my nigga?"

"While you joking, I just might be. I fucked up, man. I loved her, and I still do. I should never have listened to any of you when it came to my relationship with her. I had a good thing going with her. She was like my best friend."

Thad again sat in silence for a few minutes and decided to change the subject. "Ay, man, did you see that section in the paper about Austin's memorial?"

"Yeah, I saw something about it in the paper. They said it will be Sunday afternoon. Why, are you going?" Chris asked, looking at Thad curiously.

"Yeah, I was thinking about it. I should pay my respects. You feel me?" Thad replied.

Chris looked at Thad in amazement. Although the cops ruled his death an accident, Chris didn't feel like it was a good idea for Thad to go. "Ay, Thad, I don't think you should go. I mean, that would be kind of disrespectful, in my opinion."

"Well, I'm going, and you're coming with me, or else! Shit, I don't think we need any more bloodshed, ya feel me?" Thad murmured quietly, but not so quiet that Chris couldn't hear him or understand the meaning behind the statement.

Chris looked at Thad long and hard, until Thad threw him one of those "nigga, we got a problem" looks. Chris turned his head and looked quietly out the window. Thad laughed. "I didn't think so!"

Chris's mind filled with thoughts of how he could eject Thad from his life for good. He wasn't going to keep slick threatening his life.

Thad dropped Chris off at his car and headed to the club. He needed to relieve some stress, and what better way to do that than getting some play from his favorite stripper, Rosa. He couldn't believe that Chris had tried him about a bitch, especially one like Stephanie. He was also tripping about seeing Dana of all people. She held a lot of answers to questions, and he was going to get them. He wanted to know how Tiffany ended up at the warehouse dead and how Dana left alive. He wanted to know if Dana saw Toby there, and how he appeared when she saw him. He needed those answers!

When he parked his car outside the club, his phone rang, and as he viewed the number, he saw that it was private. He never answered private calls at all but when it called a second time he decided to see who it was. "Hello, and who the fuck is this calling me private?"

"What's up, young blood? Do you know who this is?" the person on the other end asked.

"If I knew who the hell this was I wouldn't have asked!" Thad yelled.

"I suggest you calm that tone when you speak to me. It's because of me that you're still breathing! I'm just letting you know that we are still out here and we haven't forgotten about you. Yes, you and that sweet-ass friend of yours. Time is ticking, my friend, and believe me when I say time is not on your side!"

The person started laughing, and Thad snapped, "Listen, you piece of shit, ain't no kind of bitch in me! When you get tired of playing games on this phone, come see me, bitch! You killed my brother, so I'm ready for you. I ain't hiding, my nigga, but you are and very well at that! Pussy."

Thad looked at his phone and realized that the person had hung up and probably didn't hear his outburst. If that was the case, Thad was sort of relieved. He let out an agitated breath and sat in his car, staring out into space. His brother was dead, and he was next. He wondered how life had gotten so turned around for him.

As Sunday approached, Chris was feeling more and more uncomfortable about making an appearance at the memorial. Thad called him around ten o'clock and told him that he would meet him at the plaza where the memorial was being held around eleven-thirty. Chris hesitantly agreed and hung up. He sat for a few minutes more, and then got up and started getting dressed. Chris was dressed within thirty minutes, and as he was heading out the door, his phone rang. "Hello."

"Hey, what you up to?" the caller asked.

"Shit, about to go to this memorial service in a few," he answered, smiling.

"How 'bout we meet afterward if you ain't got anything else to do?" the caller suggested.

"That's what's up. I will call you when I get back," Chris replied.

"Do that. I will be waiting for your call. See you later."

"All right, cool." Chris hung up the phone and headed out the door.

When he got to the plaza, he sat in his car listening to music and waiting for Thad to pull up. He noticed several people pulling up, and before long, the parking lot was filling up. After a few minutes more, Thad finally arrived.

The two walked into the plaza in the area where they were holding Austin's memorial. Red and white roses filled the room, and sitting on a table in the front was a gold urn with white doves engraved on it. His family sat in the front row, and they were all dressed in white, with blue and pink flowers in their hands.

Thad and Chris took a seat in the back of the room and very closely watched each individual who entered. Thad knew a few of the people who walked in, and he nodded to each one respectfully. Once everyone was seated, and the service started, Thad watched each person who held a rose stand up as the preacher spoke. They placed their roses beside the urn, and as the last person placed the final rose, the choir began to sing.

The service lasted about an hour and a half, and once it was over, everyone started exiting the building. As Thad and Chris walked out, a few people approached Thad, asking about Toby. They were wondering why he hadn't shown up. Thad made up an excuse and apologized for Toby's absence, and he rushed to his car.

The last person to walk up to them was Austin's pregnant fiancée. She hugged each of the guys. "I feel like I know you guys personally. Austin talked so much about you. I know he was an asset to you guys, but I just wanted him home at night. He was my everything. You know, a year or so ago when he first asked me to marry him, I thought about saying no. Hell, I did at first because I didn't want to stress about whether he was going to come home to me, you know, and I told him that. After a few weeks, he proposed a second time and he promised me that he was done with the street. We struggled at first, and his garage wasn't doing good at all, so I asked my father to loan us some money to stay afloat. He did, and Austin was able to gain clientele from an ad we placed. He told me that as long as we were together, he'd never be a poor man." She laughed a little bit. "I never once imagined that he would die doing something right!"

She began to cry, and a young guy walked over and put his arms around her shoulders. "Sis, come on, let's go to the car." She walked out, rambling incoherently.

Thad didn't utter a word to Chris at all before leaving. Chris frowned, not knowing what Thad was thinking, but he knew whatever it was wasn't good.

Chris brushed it off and got in his car and grabbed his phone. "I'm on my way home. Meet me there," he said before hanging up.

As he pulled away, his mind was racing a mile a minute. He had to figure out what Thad was planning.

After returning from Austin's memorial, Thad couldn't get over the many people who spoke very highly of him, and the things Austin's fiancée said. He couldn't help wondering how Austin was struggling if he had snitched on him and Toby. Toby trusted Austin, and he knew his brother's judgment of people was always on point. He saw several pictures of Austin and Toby, which crushed his heart. He sat in his room, thinking about the past. He also thought about how different things were now, and then, he began to wonder about Keith's whereabouts.

It was as if he just disappeared off the face of the earth.

He remembered that Dana had started seeing him right before he went missing. Thad couldn't help but notice that, when everything happened to them, Dana and her girls were somewhere lurking. "Maybe Austin isn't responsible for Toby's death," he thought aloud. He was beginning to feel that she might know a lot more than he realized. He was going to find out what happened to Keith, and who was really responsible for Toby's death if it was the last thing he did.

He was more determined now than ever to get to the truth of the matter. He knew he couldn't get to Ramon or Sergio, but he was going to kill whoever set them up.

Stephanie was riding Chris like a surfer hitting the waves. She had missed his dick because truth be told, he was a good fuck. She had slept with Chris three times since seeing him again.

"Damn, girl, that pussy is wet! Ride this dick, girl," Chris moaned.

"You know you got some good dick. You keep this pussy dripping. Damn, daddy, this dick is good," Stephanie said as she sat all the way up on his dick.

Chris grabbed her breasts and started massaging them as Stephanie rode him. When he felt close to cumming, he grabbed her waist and flipped her over.

"Not yet!" Stephanie groaned as Chris pulled his dick out and started eating her pussy and ass. He took his time and had Stephanie's pussy throbbing. As he felt her legs shake, he lifted up, slid his dick inside her, and started fucking her hard and fast until they both exploded.

"Damn, girl, I was surprised when you called me, and I'm glad you did. I hope you're staying the night," he said as he held Stephanie tightly.

"I'm here all night, baby. I don't have anywhere else to be, nor is there any place I'd rather be," she said as she kissed his neck.

"You want to go grab a bite to eat?" he asked.

"Let's order in. I'm good just lying here with you," she replied as she started rubbing on his dick.

Chris closed his eyes and smiled as Stephanie began to suck his dick. "Shit, round two it is!"

Once they were finished, they took a shower and ordered a pizza and wings. After the food got there, Chris said teasingly, "Dana isn't going to be mad if you stay out tonight, is she?"

Stephanie looked at him and rolled her eyes. "Fuck Dana, and who cares if she gets angry? She can't do shit to me!"

"Where the hell is Jeryca at? I haven't seen her in a long time," he continued to pry.

"That's a long story, but fuck her too," Stephanie said as she bit into a slice of pizza. Just then, her cell phone began to ring. She looked at it to see who was calling, looked back up at Chris, and then smiled and turned it off.

"If you don't mind me asking, who was that?" Chris asked, with his eyebrows drawn together.

"It was just Dana. She ain't want shit," Stephanie replied, smiling. She started thinking that she was going to milk Chris for everything she could get.

The next afternoon, Stephanie left Chris's apartment feeling quite satisfied. They had fucked two more times during the night, and she had a couple hundred dollars in her pocket. She had agreed to give it one more shot with Chris, but he had to make things up to her, which meant breaking her off that dolla-dolla bill.

Once she was in her car and pulling out of the driveway, she grabbed her phone and listened to her voicemails. One was from Dana, and the other one was from her new boo. She wasn't 'bout to let him go. He served her in every way possible. Chris was just a check to her. She immediately called her new boo back. "Hey, bae, what's up?"

"Shit, what were you doing last night where you couldn't answer my damn call?" he asked angrily.

"Baby, I got caught up with my cousin. My phone was dead as hell. We sat up talking and drinking, and after that, I went to sleep," Stephanie lied.

"Come and see me. I need you, Stephanie," he said.

"Okay, I'm on my way. Give me about forty-five minutes and I'll be there," she replied.

"All right. Hurry up," he said and then hung up.

Stephanie drove to the pharmacy and purchased a douche and a bottle of body wash. After she purchased them, she went into the women's restroom and cleaned herself up. She knew that she was going to have to fuck, and he would know that she had been having sex if she didn't do something to tighten her pussy up. She wasn't an amateur and knew exactly how to tighten it up and get it moist. That's why she used the douche.

Just as she was leaving the store, her phone beeped, alerting her that she had a text message: I don't know where you are, but you knew I had places to go today, and now I can't take care of what I need to 'cause no one is here to sit with Dana! Some friend you are!

Stephanie deleted the text immediately, fussing under her breath, "Fuck both of them hoes! I don't answer to no one!"

Chris was drying off, humming to himself, thinking about the night he had shared with Stephanie and the decision that they made to give it one more try. Chris was aware that Stephanie was probably using him in a way, but he didn't care. He knew he had to go beyond the norm and make a great effort to gain back her trust and love. He had betrayed her in so many ways before, and he vowed that he wouldn't mess up this time around. He wasn't going to let Thad get in his ear this time. He was actually growing tired of being Thad's running boy. He had to get out from under Thad's thumb. He just didn't know how.

After he got dressed, he called to check on things at the trap house, and after being told that Thad had expressed that anything going on from here on out would solely be discussed with him, Chris frowned. "Oh, really?"

"Yes. I'm not sure what's going on but until we are told differently those are the rules. I'm sorry, Chris man," said Evelyn, one of the hoes.

"That's fine. I will be over there shortly. Is he there?" Chris asked.

"Yes, he just walked in actually."

"All right. I'm on my way." Chris hung up the phone and stood there looking at it, and he started laughing.

Chris rode out to the trap house. "What's up, man?" he asked Thad as he walked into his office.

"Shit, nothing. What's up with you?" Thad asked.

"I was just informed that you didn't want any business being divulged to me anymore," Chris replied.

"Well, I assumed that you were going to be busy with your little thot and I didn't want this business to get in the way of anything," Thad said, leaning back in his chair and glaring at Chris.

"Thad, if it weren't for me, this trap house would've fallen off. I kept this shit afloat!" Chris fumed.

"I know who did what but I just figured this way would be better. Don't want any information falling in the wrong hands, if you get my drift," Thad replied.

"All right, cool. I'm out!" Chris said as he walked out without saying another word.

Chapter Eleven

Dana and Brittany were sitting on the front porch, listening to the radio. Dana's nurse had taken the day off, and Brittany was looking out for Dana. She was writing on a notepad and Dana was curious. "What you over there working on?"

"Nothing much, just thinking about starting a private law firm. I think I'm ready to get back in the mix," Brittany lied. She couldn't and wouldn't tell Dana that they were almost broke. What Brittany was actually doing was adding up the bills that she had incurred taking care of Dana.

Two weeks after their visit with Travis, and after three more doctor visits for Dana, Brittany was starting to feel the strain of taking care of Dana. Brittany didn't have any kids of her own, and in her opinion, the only family she had was Dana. From the very beginning, she felt a connection with Dana and looked at her as her younger sister. In the beginning, Brittany firmly believed that Dana had the potential to become a great attorney if she followed in her footsteps. Yes, Brittany knew that her tactics were somewhat illegal, but in her opinion, she did what she was paid to do, which was win her case.

Brittany had allowed her personal feelings for Dana to place her in situations she knew she didn't need to be in, but it was too late to worry about that. It was finished, but with the bills piling up from Dana's rehabilitation and doctors, they had to find more money to live comfortably. Brittany could've gone back to the law firm and gotten the money legitimately, but it would take too long, and they needed money ASAP.

They had already spent the money that Dana had saved up, and now Brittany's savings were dwindling. She had come up with a way to get more money, but that would consist of them pulling yet another robbery. She wasn't sure that everyone would be willing to pull another one with all the hits they'd taken on the last two robberies. She contacted Deondre and Minx and asked them to meet with her and Stephanie, who had agreed that if Brittany could convince them to participate, she would also help.

Brittany knew a guy who was a big-time drug dealer, and she also knew where he kept his money. She had gotten him off on conspiracy and intent to distribute five keys of pure cocaine. He had a safe located in his office at his estate, and he had over a million dollars in a few of his Swiss bank accounts. She had a plan to get into his safe and his accounts, but she needed backup. With Dana in a wheelchair, they had to count her out, so Brittany needed one other person to take her place. Finding that person was going to be tough.

"Oh, sounds good. Maybe I can help you, be your assistant again," Dana suggested.

"Yes, that would be great, and we can work from home, rather than going to court," Brittany replied.

"I'm getting excited!" Dana said, smiling.

Brittany hadn't seen Dana smile like that in almost two years. "If it keeps you smiling like that, then I'm definitely doing it," Brittany said, laughing.

As the two discussed the possibilities of starting a private firm, they were suddenly distracted by the report that rang out of the radio. "NYPD has just discovered a body on the outskirts of East Brooklyn. Detective Lisa Moore stated that the body has been there approximately a year and a half, and appears to be that of a female. The identity of the victim has not yet been released, pending notification of next of kin. We will bring you more information on this story as it develops."

Brittany and Dana sat speechless. They didn't know where Deondre and Minx had taken Debra's body, but they knew it was close to the east side.

"Don't say it!" Brittany said, as Dana sat up and prepared to speak.

"You don't even know what I was about to say!" Dana replied.

Brittany gave her a "yes, I do" look. "It's not her. It can't be," Brittany replied.

Dana sat back and laughed. "Well, I guess you did know."

"I got to call Minx and see what's going on," Brittany said, as she reached for her phone. "Hey, Minx, what's going on?" she asked once he picked up the phone.

"Nothing much. What's up with you? I got your message earlier today that you wanted to meet, and I was about to call you," he said.

"Okay, but that's not why I'm calling. Have you seen or listened to the news?" Brittany asked.

"No, I haven't. Why you ask that?" Minx asked.

"They have found a body over on the east side of Brooklyn. You need to get over here as soon as possible," Brittany explained.

"Okay, I can do that, but what does that have to do with me, Britt?" he asked.

Brittany exhaled sharply. "I will explain everything. Just get over here now. See if you can get in touch with Deondre and scoop him up as well," she ordered.

"All right, I will do that. See you soon," he said before hanging up.

Brittany looked at Dana and shook her head. "If it's not one thing, it's another." She wheeled Dana inside and called Stephanie. "Hey, where you at?" Brittany asked.

As Brittany talked to Stephanie, Dana could hear the agitation growing in Brittany's voice. "Look, we got an old situation that has just come up, and it involves all of us. Minx is going to try to get Deondre, and they are coming over, and I think you should too, seeing that it involves you." Brittany hung up, grabbed her hair in frustration, and screamed.

Dana had never seen Brittany so uptight. "Calm down. We don't even know if it's her. Don't panic so prematurely," Dana said quietly.

"You're right, Dana. I'm not going to freak out just yet. You want something to eat?" Brittany asked.

"No, I'm okay right now. Can we go back on the porch for a little while? I need some fresh air."

"Yeah, we can," Brittany answered.

As the two went back out, Rebecca was pulling in the driveway. "Hey, I thought you were going to be gone for a while," Brittany said as Rebecca got out and approached the porch.

"I was, but my plans changed suddenly," Rebecca said, shaking her head. She looked at Dana. "How are you feeling? You look tired."

"I am. I just got an awful headache," she explained.

"You want me to go get you an aspirin or something?" Rebecca asked.

"No, thank you."

Emily and Detective Rone decided to pay Dana another visit. They wanted to see if Dana needed anything and also if she was going to rehab like she promised them. Detective Rone also wanted to get another look at Rebecca. He couldn't shake the feeling that he had seen her somewhere before.

When they got there, everyone was sitting on the porch. Dana looked beautiful, as she always did in Detective Rone's eyes. Once they pulled into the driveway and got out of the car, Rebecca got up and walked into the house. Rone looked at Emily with an "I told you so" look, and walked toward the house.

"Good afternoon, ladies," he said as he stepped onto the porch.

"Hey, Detectives. How are you doing today?" Brittany asked.

"We're good, thanks," he answered.

"Two visits back to back. What's going on?" Dana asked suspiciously.

"Just checking to see if you kept your promise to me. You know what I'm referring to," he replied.

Dana laughed. "Yes, I went to rehab yesterday and stayed the whole time."

"Well, I'm happy to hear that." He laughed too.

"Do you have everything you need, Dana? Is there anything we can bring you?" Emily asked.

"No, I'm good. Brittany, is there anything you think we need?" Dana asked.

"Not at the moment," Brittany answered.

"Okay, well, I'm going on vacation soon, and I wanted to make sure you ladies were straight before I left," Emily explained.

"Oh, snap! Where you going?" Brittany asked.

"I'm going down South for couple of weeks. My sister is getting married, and I got to be there," Emily explained.

"Must be nice," Dana said, smiling.

As the ladies continued to talk Detective Rone asked Brittany if he could use her restroom. He walked into the house and searched the first two rooms to see if he could catch a glimpse of Rebecca. When he ventured farther into the house, he heard Rebecca's voice coming from the kitchen area: "No, I'm sure they don't expect a thing. It's okay here, but nothing compares to home."

He tiptoed away. Brittany came into the house almost yelling, "Detective Rone, I just wanted to express my sincerest thanks for coming here and checking on Dana like you do."

Detective Rone cleared his throat. "Well, uh, I'm just doing my job. But I will say this: I'm going to do everything in my power, within the law, to ensure that no one hurts her again. "

As the statement left his mouth, Rebecca walked in and quickly headed for the bedroom. Before she could disappear, Detective Rone called out to her, "Excuse me. Where are you from, if you don't mind me asking?"

"Detective Rone, you are always in business mode. Trust I had her thoroughly investigated before I hired her," Brittany assured him as she ushered him out the front door. She needed to get rid of him before Stephanie and the guys pulled up.

"Well, Dana, do you need anything before we leave? Because I'm getting the impression that we aren't wanted right now." He laughed.

"No, I'm good for now. But, Emily, come see me before you leave for your vacation," Dana said.

"I sure will. Y'all take care," Emily replied.

"All right," Brittany said with a bright, fake smile.

Once Detective Rone and Detective Jackson were in the car, he fastened his seat belt and looked over at her. "Something is definitely up. I don't know what it is, but I'm gonna find out."

Forty-five minutes after Detective Rone and Emily left, Deondre and Minx were pulling in the driveway and Stephanie wasn't too far behind. Once everyone was inside, Brittany filled everyone in on what had just been announced on the radio.

She looked at Minx. "Where did you bury Debra?"

"To be honest, Britt, we didn't go with Zack to dispose of the body, but we did place her body in a barrel and placed bricks in it to weigh her down. I don't know how it could've resurfaced," Minx explained.

"Hold up, what do you mean you didn't go with Zack to get rid of the body? That was all you had to do! Now look at what's going on! Dammit!" Brittany yelled.

"Look, Britt, Zack told us he had it covered; that he knew a good location where she would never be found. We trusted that nigga's word," Minx explained further.

Brittany sighed. "I understand. I'm just tripping right now. We got to come up with a plan to cover our asses, just in case."

After the group talked for an hour or so, they came up with a plan to just say nothing. If they didn't have evidence, then they weren't going to say shit.

After everyone left, Dana went to bed, and Brittany sat on the porch for a little while, trying to get her thoughts together and come up with a master plan.

Detective Lisa Moore had just walked into the precinct after visiting the Fuller family and delivering the devastating news that they had found the body of their daughter, Debra. She had been missing for over a year, and they received a tip from an anonymous caller. It took them about two hours to find the huge oil drum that they were advised they would find the body in. They immediately loaded the oil drum in the crime scene van and transported it to the lab. To her surprise, whoever killed her had left her purse next to her body, so it was easy to identify her. Debra had also had a breast implant procedure done, and they were able to confirm her identity from their serial numbers as well.

Detective Moore walked into her office after finishing up yet another press conference, and she sat down, exhausted, in her chair. She leaned back and threw her head backward. She closed her eyes and thought about the case before her, but before she could get too deep in thought, there was a knock at the door. "Come in!" she yelled.

Officer Harris, Detective Rone's old partner, walked in. "How are you doing, Detective Moore?" he asked.

"I'm okay. And what can I do for you, Officer Harris?" she asked, immediately killing the small talk.

He sat down across from her. "Well, I heard that you guys found Debra Fuller's body and I have some information that may be valuable to you," he replied.

"Yes, we did. What information do you have?" she asked.

"When I was working with Detective Rone, we had information leaked to us that Dana Crisp and Brittany Howell were involved in Debra Fuller's kidnapping. However, when we followed up after a few days, we spoke with Ms. Fuller, and she informed us that she was okay."

"Is that right? I wonder why Detective Rone hasn't come forward with that piece of information himself," she said more to herself than to Officer Harris.

"I thought you should know that they were previously investigated for kidnapping," Officer Harris continued.

"Thank you for that tidbit of information, and I will follow up on it immediately. Have a great day," Lisa stated, dismissing him, as she started flipping through her paperwork.

Officer Harris sat there for a moment, trying to figure out why Lisa Moore was being so rude to him. He had just given her a huge piece of information, and she brushed it and him off, as well as calling what he gave her a "tidbit"!

Lisa looked up at him. "Is there anything else, Officer?"

Harris smiled and shook his head. "Nothing else." He stood up and walked out of her office. He then leaned up against the wall and shook with anger. *I bet I won't offer that bitch any more information.*

As he started walking down the hall, he bumped into Detective Rone. "How are you doing, old man?"

"I'm good, young blood. It's been a while. How you been doing?" Detective Rone asked.

"I been good. Just trying to make it off of these few pennies I'm making now," Officer Harris replied.

"Well, you know you can come back over to the squad, become a detective again. We need you, and the pay is a li'l greater, but you already know that," Rone suggested.

"Yeah, but I think I'm good where I'm at. I don't have the desire to deal with all the things you guys do. I'm actually thinking about a new career change altogether," Harris explained.

"Really? What are you going to do?" Rone asked.

"I haven't decided yet, but whatever I do, it's got to bring in more money than this job. I think I already got something lined up, and if that doesn't work, I'm hoping I hit the lottery!" Harris laughed.

Rone looked at Harris and wondered what he was up to. His body movement and whole demeanor was odd. "So, what brings you over to this side?"

"Oh, uh," Harris stammered, "just thought I'd come pay my favorite people a visit. You know I miss y'all."

"Yeah. Well, I'ma go on down here and take care of a few things in my office. Take care, Harris, and I wish you luck on that lottery win," Rone said as he reached out to shake Harris's hand.

"All right, old timer. See you around," Harris replied, shaking Rone's hand before walking off.

Once Detective Rone was in his office, he stood in front of a picture on his wall. It was of him and Harris. He shook his head, again wondering what Harris was up to. Then he looked at the case files on his desk from the day before.

"This is a never-ending job," he whispered.

Back in her office, Lisa wrote down everything that Harris had just shared with her. She decided to contact Detective Rone and find out why he hadn't come forward with the information himself. Something just didn't sit right with her, and she was going to get to the bottom of it if it was the last thing she did.

She looked over the coroner's results and saw that the cause of death was undetermined. She had her work cut out for her, but she'd promised the Fuller family justice, and she aimed to keep her promise to them.

She laughed aloud as she recalled the look on Harris's face when she sent him on his way. "Crazy li'l shit think he did something," she mumbled softly. She would've gotten that information without his meddling ass.

Chapter Twelve

Jeryca woke up Saturday morning with Farrah heavily on her mind. She owed Farrah so much in so many ways that not even Stephanie or Dana could imagine. Orlando had torn into her yet again the night before about money issues, but she had to send Shirley something to help with Travis. She was going to send her some money anonymously. She hadn't spoken to her in a long time, but she had kept in touch through Pam, by having her drop by occasionally to see them. Pam would also babysit Travis every now and then to give Shirley a much-needed break. The last time Pam visited, she learned that Shirley was running low on money and had sold Farrah's bracelet to pay for Travis's counseling session. Jeryca wouldn't sit idly by and see her struggle. Orlando could get mad all he wanted, but she was sending $20,000 by Priority Mail.

As she lay back in the tub and closed her eyes, she started thinking back to when Greg was in her mother's life. Although her mother had sent Greg packing after she'd caught him trying to rape Jeryca, she brought him back into their lives just a few months later. Sheila had told Jeryca that she needed Greg in a way she couldn't understand, and he'd promised her that he was going to change.

Jeryca remembered how uncomfortable she felt coming home after school or just being in his presence. He hadn't said a word to her, but every now and then, she caught him watching her. One day after school, Jeryca had walked into her house thinking that she was there alone, but as she lay across her bed to do her homework, she heard a sound behind her. She turned around, and once again, Greg had intruded into her room. "Daddy's home!" he'd growled, laughing. "This time we won't be interrupted. You caused me a lot of grief the last time, and the way I see it, you owe me. And I'm here to collect."

Greg definitely had been drunk, because Jeryca could smell the wine on his breath, and his words were slurred. As he'd advanced upon her, she jumped up and started screaming. Greg ran up on her, covered her mouth with one hand, and held her arm with the other, forcing her backward until she felt her back hit the wall.

"Uh-uh, don't do that, Jeryca. See, you trying to put everybody in our business, and I won't have that this time. Now, give daddy some of that sweet sugar!" he had whispered, as he began kissing her neck. Jeryca had squirmed and mumbled her protests, but Greg wasn't paying her pleas any attention.

Finally, for a split second, Jeryca's struggles had set her free, only to have her hemmed up yet again as she raced toward the door. Her lamp fell from the nightstand and crashed to the floor, which caused a loud thudding sound to echo through the house. As they wrestled, they were unaware of a third person entering the room. Greg had slammed Jeryca on the bed, and he started writhing in pain no sooner than they landed.

Standing over him was Farrah with the fallen lamp. She had hit Greg repeatedly across the head and back area until he collapsed on the floor. Jeryca had jumped up and run to Farrah, and the two girls left the apartment. A few minutes later they sat in the park, talking. Jeryca was shaken up, and Farrah was doing her best to console her friend. They were both very young at the time, but it was a memory that Jeryca would always cherish, because her friend had come to her rescue.

Jeryca was suddenly jolted back to the present as Orlando stumbled into the house and then crashed through the bedroom door. Jeryca sat up, frightened, and quickly got out of the tub.

When she got to him, she saw that he'd fallen. "Are you okay, baby?" she asked as she bent down to help him sit up. She didn't miss the odor of liquor on his breath.

"I'm all right!" he slurred as he tried unsuccessfully to get up several times. He finally allowed Jeryca to help him up, and he leaned on her as she helped him to the bed. As he fell backward, he covered his head and looked at Jeryca. "You're going to be the death of me!"

Jeryca stood staring at him as his snoring filled the room. She didn't know what to think about what he had just said.

She called Pam after she took Orlando's shoes off. Thinking about Farrah had her wondering how Travis was doing. Pam agreed to go over and check on them, as she always did.

Once Pam arrived at Shirley's house, Travis ran and dived in her lap, almost toppling her over. Pam started laughing and playfully slammed him. Of everyone who visited him, Pam was the only one who roughhoused him. She didn't baby him as the others did. She was great with him, and Shirley definitely noticed it. She loved the way Pam interacted with Travis, and although Pam was strict when he wanted to be babied, Travis respected her and loved her.

Shirley had fixed dinner and asked Pam if she wanted to stay. At first, she declined, but after several "please stay's" from Travis, she agreed.

"Stop that whining, boy! I'ma stay, but you got to promise to show me how much of a big boy you can be when I get ready to leave."

"But—" he started, Pam instantly stopped him.

"Nope! No whining, Travis. You a big boy and you got to act like a big boy. You understand?"

"Yes," he answered, with his head bowed.

After they ate dinner, Pam read Travis his favorite book, *The Three Little Pigs*. He laid his head on her lap and rubbed her thumb. That one gesture pulled at Pam's heart because it made her feel truly loved unconditionally.

While Pam read to Travis, Shirley cleaned the kitchen. She felt at ease, knowing Pam was there.

Pam sat for a few minutes more and then stood up. "Give me a hug, li'l man."

Travis started to protest, but Pam reminded him of the promise that he had made. Shirley walked her to the door and out onto the porch.

"I talked to Jeryca, and she wanted me to let you guys know that she loves you all and will be sending you a package soon," Pam said, as she started walking down the steps.

"I really do appreciate both of you girls. If it weren't for Jeryca sending me the money she does each month, I don't know what we would do. She is a jewel. Next time you talk to her, tell her to call me soon. Okay?"

"Okay, I will. Y'all have a blessed night," Pam said, as she walked down the street.

She approached the bus stop and heard a horn blowing loudly behind her. She turned as the car was pulling over. For a brief moment, Pam froze up, until she saw Stephanie getting out of the car.

"Hey, sis, long time no see," she said, walking toward her with her arms outstretched.

Stephanie hugged her, but it wasn't real, and Pam felt it. However, Pam had no idea that Jeryca had betrayed Stephanie and Dana. All she knew was that Jeryca moved to Miami with her rich boyfriend to make a better life for herself.

"You talk to Jeryca lately?" Stephanie asked.

"Yeah, I have. She is doing okay," Pam said, remembering that Jeryca told her not to tell anyone where she was, not even Stephanie or Dana. She told her that Orlando didn't want her to communicate with them anymore, because of their way of life. Pam didn't think it was cool to diss her friends for a man, but she assumed that Jeryca knew what she was doing, and she wasn't in any position to question her sister's decision.

"Oh, and where is she? Girl, we miss her like crazy," Stephanie said, looking weirdly at Pam.

Pam wasn't feeling the vibe that Stephanie was putting out, and she decided that she should end the conversation immediately. "Girl, I don't know exactly where she is, but I really have to go."

"Wait a minute. I can take you home if you like. Ain't no need in waiting on the bus," Stephanie said as she stepped in Pam's way, blocking her from walking away.

"Um, well, I have someone waiting for me at the bus depot, so I can't take you up on your offer today," Pam answered quickly.

Stephanie took a step forward. "You sure? I mean, I can take you where you need to go. You're family."

"No, I'm good, but thanks. Come by the house and see me sometime," Pam said as she walked toward the bus, which had just pulled up.

"All right then. Next time you talk to Jeryca, tell her I said hello and she should come on back home."

"I will tell her. Bye."

Stephanie watched Pam get on the bus and then she walked to her car. She sat there for a second before cranking it up and pulling off.

Jeryca was sitting on her bed, listening to Pam tell her about her visit with Travis and the weird encounter with Stephanie. Jeryca frowned after Pam explained how weird Stephanie had been acting. It never occurred to her that her baby sister would be caught up in the midst of all the drama she had left behind. She would fuck those hoes over in the worst way if they harmed one hair on Pam's head.

"Where is Mom at?" Jeryca asked.

"In her room with Todd, as usual. He is still trying to get her to ask you for money. She said she would come up with it some other way, but he ain't trying to hear it. He said he know you and your man got it, and he need a few thousand or he will be killed. He owes some kind of gambling debt, I guess," Pam answered.

"Go tell her to come to the phone, please," Jeryca replied.

Pam sighed. "She is going to cuss me out if I knock on her door, Jeryca."

"Just go do what I asked," Jeryca ordered.

"Okay, I'm going," Pam said. She slowly walked out of her room to her mother's door.

Pam knocked on the door twice before it was jerked open by Todd. "Don't you fucking hear us in here talking? You are the most disrespectful bitch I know!" he growled.

Pam looked at her mother expecting her to stand up to him and cuss him out for calling her out her name, but she sat in her lounge chair in a daze. Pam shook her head. "Mom, telephone."

"Dammit, Sheila, will you please tell her to go back in her room? We are trying to have a conversation!" Todd yelled.

"Pam, tell your mother to get her ass on the fucking phone now!" Jeryca was seething with anger after hearing the way Todd was talking to Pam.

"Mother, Jeryca wants to speak with you now," Pam said, trying once more to get her mom to the phone.

"Tell her I will call her tomorrow. I am not in the mood to speak to her tonight," Sheila mumbled.

"Did you hear that, Jeryca? Do you see what I mean now?" Pam asked as she walked back into her room and closed her door quietly. Pam soon finished her call with Jeryca and went to bed.

Pam left for school feeling tired and disgusted. Todd had cussed her mother out for not talking to Jeryca, knowing that he needed money. After the two argued they fucked, and she had spent most of her night listening to her mom moaning and screaming, "Fuck me, Mr. Tibs," into the wee hours of the morning. It was as if she forgot that she had an impressionable teenager sleeping in the next room. She knew that Jeryca was angry that her mother didn't get on the phone or stand up for her when Todd called her a bitch. Jeryca swore that she was going to get her away from Brooklyn soon, but Pam had her doubts. She felt all alone, with no friends to talk to.

Pam walked into her classroom and was immediately sent to the principal's office. She sat on the bench and waited for him to call her in his office.

"Pam Mebane, come on into my office, please," the principal said as he opened the door. Pam walked in and was greeted by an officer.

"Hi, Ms. Mebane. I'm Detective Rone, and I need to talk to you about your sister, Jeryca Mebane."

"I don't know what I can do to help you. We haven't heard from Jeryca in over a year. She and my mom fell out when I was in the hospital, and she has been MIA since," Pam replied, looking Detective Rone in the eyes, lying with every word she spoke.

"Before she disappeared, did she mention travelling anywhere or mention having issues with Dana Crisp?" he asked.

Pam sat back and frowned. "No, she didn't, and why are you asking me about my sister harming Dana? They were friends, and she wouldn't hurt any of them. Shouldn't my mother be here, Detective Rone? I have nothing else to say."

"You are free to go at any time. We just need to find your sister now. If you hear anything, here is my card. I will contact your mother and set up a time to talk with you again," Detective Rone said, as he handed the card to Pam. He walked out of the office.

Pam walked to her class, wondering why he'd asked her about Jeryca harming Dana. She remembered how Stephanie was acting when she last saw her, and she knew something was stinking among her sister and her two friends.

Chapter Thirteen

Chris had avoided Thad's phone calls for a few days, and he finally decided it was time to call him back. "Hey, what's going on, man?" he asked, once Thad answered the phone.

"Well, damn, I thought I was going to have to send a search party out looking for you. What you been up to?" Thad asked suspiciously.

Chris sat quietly for a minute before speaking. "Well, I've been seeing someone and been spending time with them since I have no job now."

"Shit, you know I been in my feelings with everything that's been going on, and then to see and learn that you kicking it with Stephanie kind of made me feel some kind of way. Hell, you know I been thinking about Jeryca ass lately a little bit. They did bring some kind of excitement with them, didn't they?" Thad asked.

Chris laughed. "Yes, they did. I'll see you soon, Thad. What you got going on today?"

"Nothing at all. 'Bout to head into the city. You know, they having that Day in the Park at

Brooklyn Bridge Park. Shit, I might meet my next thugette." Thad laughed.

"I know that's right. I'ma meet you there then," Chris said.

"That's what's up! Let's turn up at the park," Thad replied.

Chris felt as if he was talking to the old Thad. He wondered when the change occurred. He could deal with this Thad.

Thad got dressed and headed to the park. He needed to relax and clear his mind. His days had been consumed with revenge, mourning, and hatred. He was ready for a small change. Live jazz music and being surrounded by people who were enjoying life was exactly what he needed.

When he arrived at the park, there were no parking areas available, so he had to park a block away and walk down, which he didn't mind. The air was cool and crisp, and the music was bumping loud from the park. He passed a few beautiful women, but none of them were really the thugettes he was looking for. He checked his phone to see if Chris had called. Seeing that he hadn't yet, he continued into the park. "What a gorgeous day," he muttered.

Detective Rone dropped Emily off at the airport and decided to call and check on Dana.

With the way Brittany and Rebecca were acting when he last visited, he decided he was going to check in on Dana more often.

He dialed the house number and was about to hang up when Dana answered, "Hello?"

"Hey, Dana, this is Detective Rone. How is everything over there?"

"It's going okay. Just wish I could get out of this house," she replied.

"Brittany won't take you out for a while?" he asked.

"She isn't here, and neither is Stephanie. But I'm good, Detective Rone."

"Where is your nurse? She can't take you out for a while?" he asked, prying a bit.

"Today is her day off, and she is going out in a little bit," Dana answered.

"Well, I'm in your area, and I can stop by and take you out if you would like. I don't like the thought of you being there by yourself," he told her.

"I'll be okay, but thanks anyway. Look, I'm going to get off the phone and lie down for a little while. I got a slight headache. Thanks for calling, though," she said as she concluded her call.

Detective Rone hung up and headed toward Dana's way anyway. He figured since he was close by he could check Rebecca out a bit. Dana had just said she was going to be leaving soon, and he could follow her and see where she was going.

He drove quickly to Dana's road and pulled back into a side road and watched Dana's house. He saw that Rebecca's car was still in the yard, and a few minutes later, Brittany arrived. Rebecca left moments later.

Detective Rone tailed Rebecca for about five miles. She slowed down and turned into a huge parking lot. Detective Rone frowned as he realized they were at the rehabilitation center that Dana was going to.

"What is she doing here without Dana?" he wondered aloud.

He pulled in across the street at a store and watched. Thirty minutes later she emerged, pushing someone in a wheelchair.

"That must be another patient of hers," he thought at first. He couldn't get a good look at the person at first, but as Rebecca pushed them to the passenger side door and wheeled them around to get them in the car, Detective Rone almost choked on the water he was drinking. He couldn't believe what he was seeing, who he was seeing. He finally remembered how he knew Rebecca and who she was!

His first instinct was to call Brittany and tell her he needed to talk to her. But he dismissed that idea quickly. He couldn't understand why Brittany would hire that woman if she had truly run a thorough background check on her. It wasn't adding up. Detective Rone decided that he would wait to talk to Brittany and do his own research.

He called the precinct and talked to his pal of twenty years to get him to run a background check on both Brittany and Rebecca for him. He needed answers immediately. It was the only way he was going to rest. He couldn't wait to tell Emily what he had just discovered.

He knew she was still on the plane, but he dialed her number and left her a message: "Hey, this is Rone. Call me as soon as you get this! You aren't going to believe what I've just discovered." He hung up and continued to watch as Rebecca kissed the person on the forehead, shut the door, walked to the driver's side, and got in. Once she pulled off, Detective Rone was on her tail. He was going to follow her all day if he had to. He had nothing but time.

Brittany and Dana were doing a few exercises on Dana's legs. "All right, Dana you're doing great today! I'm so proud of the progress you're making. I knew you had it in you!" Brittany praised her.

"Yeah, I got to get out of this chair. You were right, Britt: I can't continue to sulk around and feel sorry for myself. I got to get back to my old self. I'm very thankful for having you and Stephanie with me. I love you guys so much. You know, when I was a little girl I used to dream of making it big as an actress, but as I got older and saw friends and family get railroaded by the system, law became my reality. Never once did I dream that I'd be this person," Dana said as she waved her hand downward toward her legs.

"The person you are is great. You made a few misjudgments, and hell, so did I for that matter, but we both made our decisions, and it's too late to change them. We just got to deal with it the best we can. I'm here for you," Brittany replied.

"You think I got one more set of ten leg lifts in me?" Dana asked, smiling.

"Hell yeah, let's get it!" Brittany said, smiling.

Monday morning, Dana was dropped off at the rehabilitation center early. Brittany told her she had some business to take care of, and as of late, Stephanie was nowhere to be found. Rebecca hadn't shown up to work in two days, which had everyone on edge. Dana didn't really care if she returned. She just hated putting more problems on Brittany.

Dana wondered why Brittany was in a such a rush that morning. Brittany had gotten a phone call early that morning that seemed to disturb her, and she wasn't very talkative at all. Dana was working on the FES bicycle. Because of the little leg movement she had, the machine allowed her to pedal a stationary cycle called an ergometer. Mild electrical pulses helped her leg muscles contract, which let her pedal.

She was on the bicycle for about twenty minutes when her heart felt as if it would burst in her chest, and her eyes collided with another patient who was being wheeled in.

Brenda!

Dana stared into the eyes of the woman she had attempted to kill over a year ago. Brenda smiled and turned her head. Dana sat confused, unable to think straight. *I thought she was dead!* She whispered to herself, "What else can go wrong?"

No sooner than she asked, Detective Moore walked in with two other cops behind her. Dana dropped her head and saw them walking over to Brenda.

Fuck. They're 'bout to take my ass to jail. Fuck, man! Dana began to hyperventilate when she saw them all look in her direction. *Calm down, Dana.* As the police headed in her direction, Dana began to silently pray.

"Ms. Dana Crisp?" Detective Moore asked as she approached, flashing her badge.

"Yes, I'm Dana. What can I do for you?" Dana replied, trying to keep cool.

"I'm Detective Moore, and I'd like to ask you a few questions about one Debra Fuller."

"I'm not sure how I can assist you, but ask your questions," Dana said.

"When was the last time you saw or spoke to her?" Detective Moore asked.

"It's been over a year now. We used to work together. I hope everything is all right," Dana said.

"Ma'am, Miss Debra Fuller was found dead a few days ago, and I was given the case. I went over a file that Detective Rone had on her, and I saw where you and Brittany were questioned about her disappearance. You know what else I do recall? That happened around the same time that Brenda over there"—Detective Moore nodded in Brenda's direction—"was shot. You know she almost died. It's a damn shame she has no memory of what happened. I'd love to find out who shot her as well. But listen to me, jumping all off the subject. Do you by any chance remember the exact day that you last saw her? What she had on? What her demeanor was?"

"I can't recall. I've been through a lot myself lately, so I really don't think I can help you," Dana responded as she started the machine back up.

Taking that as her cue that the conversation was over, Detective Moore reached in her pocket, took out a card, and handed it to Dana. "If you remember anything please give me a call."

"Sure," Dana said, as Detective Moore watched Dana place the card on top of her belongings that sat in her wheelchair.

As the officers left the building, Dana let out a calming breath of air. She had just learned two things that eased her mind just a bit: one, they didn't have any idea who killed Debra, and two, Brenda couldn't remember who she was. She smiled, but as she looked over, she saw Brenda watching her. It was eerie and uneasiness set in her once again.

Thirty minutes later, Stephanie was there to get her.

"Damn, bitch, where the fuck you been hiding?" Dana asked.

"I had a few things to take care of, boo. I called Brittany, and she told me you were here, and she asked if I could pick you up. You ready?" Stephanie answered.

"Yeah, I'm ready. Look over to your right and tell me who you see," Dana said under her breath.

Stephanie looked over and froze for a minute. "Well, damn, is that—"

"Yes, bitch, it is!" Dana said before Stephanie could finish her question.

"She's looking over here like she lost something," Stephanie said, obviously aggravated.

"They said she doesn't remember anything before the shooting, but she keeps eyeing me like she remembers something," Dana whispered.

"Well, let's not worry about her too much. Listen, they are having Day in the Park today at Brooklyn Bridge Park. Do you want to go with me?" Stephanie asked.

"I don't know," Dana answered. "That's so far away."

"Girl, come on. You ain't got nothing else to do, so we might as well have a little fun. Brittany said she is going to be out of touch for a while today, so let's do something other than sit at the house," Stephanie said.

"Okay, Steph, let's go. You are right. I can't keep hiding in the house. I think that's a great idea. Hey, I've got an idea: let's go get Travis," Dana said.

Stephanie started pushing Dana out of the rehab center, but not without giving Brenda one last glance over as they walked by. To her astonishment, Brenda smiled and nodded.

"Yeah, that bitch acting real suspect," Stephanie said once they were outside.

"I told you!" Dana replied.

As the two girls hit the expressway and headed to Shirley's house, Dana relaxed and was ready to see Travis. She didn't see him as often as she used to or call as much, but she did love him. She just felt awkward being around them, knowing what she had done. Truth be told, every day Dana regretted killing Farrah. She knew that Farrah had been under extreme pressure and she only did what any mother would do, which was keep her child by any means necessary. "It should've been Jeryca's ass!" Dana said aloud unknowingly.

"What you say about Jeryca?" Stephanie asked.

"Nothing, just thinking about my current situation," Dana replied.

Stephanie didn't utter a word.

When they approached the exit to Shirley's house, Dana looked at her watch. They had left the rehab center at nine-thirty, and now it was eleven. *We made real good time.*

When they pulled up to the house, Stephanie went in to see if they could take Travis to the park. When she emerged with a jumpy Travis, Dana smiled and waved at Shirley.

"Thanks for taking Travis out with you. I been wondering when he was going to see you again. He has been worrying me to death about you two," Shirley yelled.

"These doctor visits have been consuming a lot of my time, but we couldn't come down this way without seeing our little man," Dana replied.

Travis got into the back seat and put his seat belt on. "I'm ready, Auntie Steph. Hey, Auntie Dana, you look very pretty today."

"Why, thank you, baby," Stephanie replied. "You look handsome yourself."

"You ready for a fun day at the park?" Dana asked excitedly.

"Yahhh!" Travis squealed.

"All right, let's get it then." Dana laughed.

Thirty minutes later, they arrived at the park and Stephanie was thrilled to see that it was a nice turnout. She helped Travis out of the car first and opened up her trunk to get Dana's wheelchair out. As she was pulling the chair out, she heard a soft whistle behind her.

"Looking good, babe," a familiar voice called out.

"Well, what are you doing here, Deondre?" she asked.

"The same thing you are, I'm guessing. You need any help getting Dana out?" he asked.

"Yes, please," Stephanie said as she stepped a little bit to the side, allowing Deondre to open up the wheelchair.

"Dana, I'm surprised but happy to see that you are out and about today," he said as he opened her door and helped her stand up. After he assisted her into her chair, they headed off into the park.

Deondre pushed Dana with Stephanie by his side, and the three of them laughed and talked. Travis was having a good time as well. He rode a few of the rides and happily asked Stephanie to get on the carousel with him. They ate hot dogs, and Deondre bought Travis some cotton candy, which he had all around his mouth.

As they moved around the park and took a seat on the bench next to the creek, Dana heard Travis yell, "There go my Uncle Chris and T!"

She turned and looked and before her eyes was Chris, with Thad next to him. Deondre excused himself, as he didn't want to cause any problems, especially with Travis there.

"Hello, ladies," Thad said, eyeing Dana.

Keeping it civil, Dana smiled. "Hello, Thad. How are you?"

"I've been good," he replied.

"That's great," she said coolly.

"You're looking good," Thad said.

"Thank you. And you're looking"—Dana looked him over—"like yourself."

Thad laughed. "I guess I do."

The two were so busy trying to be nice to each other, they hadn't noticed that Stephanie and Chris had walked off with Travis, and were heading back on the carousel.

"Well, it looks like it's just you and me, Miss Lady." Thad laughed.

Dana looked at him long and hard. "I guess it is."

Thad and Dana spent the remainder of their time at the park talking. Dana figured she could tolerate him just for a little while.

Later that afternoon, Dana and Stephanie dropped Travis off and headed back down the highway to go home. Neither of them spoke. Dana pretended that she was asleep because she wanted to avoid any questions that Stephanie may have had concerning what she and Thad had talked about.

Once Stephanie arrived at home, she was glad to see that Brittany's car was parked in the driveway. She promised Chris that she would meet him at his place once Brittany arrived to sit with Dana. She pushed Dana into the house and called out for Brittany.

Brittany emerged from the kitchen with her apron on, and in her hand was a spoon that was covered in sauce. "Where have you two been?" she asked, smiling.

"We went and picked up Travis and went to Day in the Park," Dana replied, smiling.

"Oh, yeah, how was it?" Brittany asked.

"Shit, girl, it was lovely, but guess who mysteriously showed up?" Dana questioned with a smirk and side-eye at Stephanie.

"Who?" Brittany asked, looking from Dana to Stephanie.

"Chris and Thad were there. But it was a coincidence, Dana!" Stephanie replied, looking at Dana and frowning.

"Humph, aren't we being touchy about the Chris subject? You were all in his ass at the park," Dana replied snottily.

"Well, Dana, you didn't seem to mind it while we were at the park, so why speak on it now?" Stephanie asked in an agitated manner.

"I'm just telling Brittany what happened at the park, Stephanie, don't get so offended. Damn," Dana said, rolling her eyes.

"Man, whatever. I'm getting ready to go! I will see y'all later," Stephanie replied, as she headed for her room.

Dana started laughing, which caused Stephanie to pause and look back at Dana. "You were looking quite chummy with Thad at one point, Dana. Is that li'l twat getting heated to the point that you will fuck with Jeryca's old flame?"

Dana looked at Stephanie and laughed. "Bitch, I told you, I was just telling Brittany what we did today. Don't get no attitude with me! I swear, you lucky I'm in this chair!"

"You ain't talking 'bout shit, 'cause even out that chair you couldn't fuck with me on my worst day and you know it. Don't think 'cause I'm Caucasian I couldn't beat yo' ass, Dana," Stephanie said as she took a step forward.

"Hey, now, you two chill out. It ain't that serious, for real. Whatever you and Chris got going on is your business. I think Dana was just joking," Brittany said, stepping in front of Stephanie. "I mean, I would've never asked about y'all's day if I knew it was going to lead to this."

Stephanie turned without saying a word and walked into her room. She grabbed a few of her personal items and walked out of the house.

After Chris left the park, he and Thad went and grabbed them a bite to eat, and they discussed how great Dana appeared to be doing. Thad kept throwing shots at him about Stephanie, but he ignored it. He wasn't trying to argue with Thad, period. However, what really caught his attention was a comment Thad made about himself and Dana. He'd said that he wouldn't mind chopping up a few grand with her in the near future.

Chris wondered why Thad would make such a comment after seeing and talking to Dana on only two occasions, unless something more was going on between the two that they weren't telling. He was going to check with Stephanie once he fucked her a few times, and see if she had noticed any difference in Dana's conversations about Thad.

Chris arrived at the hotel and started getting fresh for his night with Stephanie. He hadn't seen her in a few days, which had him wondering where she had been, but he wasn't going to ruin his night with her by asking any questions. He had his CD player, champagne, scented candles, massage oils, weed, and some strawberries. He was going to make this night memorable.

Chris showered and lay across the bed and took a short nap while waiting for Stephanie. About an hour later, Stephanie was walking into the room. He sat up and stared at her as she undressed.

She said, "I'll be right back. I'ma take me a quick shower and change into something more comfortable."

Stephanie got into the shower and thought about what had transpired between her and Dana. The situation could've very well gotten out of hand. Stephanie sighed as the hot water attacked her body, which comforted her immensely. She stayed in the shower about five minutes, and when she emerged from the restroom, Chris was happy to see her wearing nothing at all. She smiled as she walked over to her bag and pulled out a pair of fuzzy handcuffs, a feathered whip, and a CD.

As she got situated, Chris lit the candles and placed the champagne on the nightstand, along with the strawberries and oil. Stephanie crawled on the bed and pushed Chris backward. She placed his hands above his head and handcuffed them to the headboard.

Once she finished, she got up and turned the CD on, and as Minnie Riperton's "Inside My Love" sang out, Stephanie slowly danced over to the bed, never taking her eyes off Chris. As she climbed on top of him, she kissed his lips as her hips rotated against his pelvis, causing his dick to spring to attention. She grabbed her feather whip and rubbed it across Chris's chest, and as he closed his eyes, she lightly tapped him with it, causing him to thrust upward. A moan escaped his lips. Stephanie played with him a few seconds more, grabbed a piece of ice, placed it between her lips, and rubbed it across each one of Chris's nipples. They hardened immediately, just as his dick had.

Stephanie sat up and smiled. She grabbed one of the candles and poured some of the hot liquid over Chris's chest down toward his navel. The burning sensation was intense, but it was a feeling that turned Chris on even more.

Stephanie followed up by pouring a small amount of champagne over the wax to cool it down. Pre-cum immediately began oozing from his rock-hard dick. Stephanie again smiled as she noticed the wetness.

She quickly removed his handcuffs. He grabbed her by the waist and started moving her ass back and forth so that she could feel how hard his dick really was. He moved his hands upward and started to caress her firm breasts. He flipped her onto her back and started kissing her on her neck, moving downward and giving extra kisses to her tits. Finally, he nestled his head in between her thighs and planted light kisses on them. He rose up, reached for a strawberry, and placed it in the center of her pussy. As he ate and sucked the strawberry out of her, he had to admit that he never tasted a strawberry that delicious before.

Stephanie was squirming under him from the pleasure of what he was doing, and as Gerald Levert then sang out from the CD player, the two made love into the wee hours of the morning.

Chapter Fourteen

Sergio and Ramon met with the other heads of the family and discussed several subjects. Orlando and Jeryca were at the top of the list. They had to get the money that was owed to them or get rid of Jeryca and Orlando for good. They also knew that although Zack was loyal to them, he was just as loyal to Orlando.

"These guys have made a lot of money for us and moved triple the amount of guns and drugs than any man we've bought on board. Maybe we can give Orlando a little more time to get us what he owes," Ramon suggested.

"How much time do you propose we give him? We have already extended him two months to get us the money that he owes us, and he has yet to produce a dime. Now I know you have formed a bond with him, but let's not forget that we run a business and the money that they owe us is revenue for our company," one of the elders replied.

"But they bring in a ton of money for us. Who would we get to make us profit like they do? Even with the money he owes us, he still has put millions in our pockets," Ramon said, continuing to plead Orlando's case.

A second gentleman spoke up: "Ramon, have you gone soft on us? Do we need to replace you? It's not like Orlando is in debt to us by a few measly hundred dollars! He owes us hundreds of thousands. That's the difference. Now either he gives us the money that is owed, or he will die. I want the best guys on it. We got to keep our reputation intact. If anyone suspects that we have allowed someone on our team to get away with stealing from us—and you know that's what they have done—then everyone will try us and that I will not have! You two have done a great job keeping things together. Don't slip up now because you feel some kind of way about the boy."

"No one has gone soft, and our feelings aren't involved at all, but like Ramon said, Father, it just makes more sense to keep them on board. Let's make him work a couple of runs for us for free until we get what's owed to us. We can't keep killing people when there are obviously other methods to get our money," Sergio finally spoke up.

After a few minutes of deliberation, the crew decided that they would give Orlando one more opportunity to pay his debt, but if he failed they would have him killed. They also ordered Sergio to find out all he could about Orlando and Jeryca. They wanted to know everything about their past, next of kin, jail records; anything that they could dig up, they were ordered to collect. When the elders made their demands, they were to be carried out. Family or not, any disobedience of any kind resulted in deadly repercussions.

While Ramon was putting a call through to Orlando, who immediately agreed to make a few runs without pay, Sergio placed a call to a few of his friends in Brooklyn who could give him all the background information he needed on Orlando and Jeryca. He prayed that Orlando didn't let them down. He also gathered background information on Zack, because he knew that Zack wouldn't be okay with Orlando being murdered.

Back in Brooklyn, Monday Night

Pam sat in her room after she got home from school. Her mother was in one of her moods, so she decided to avoid her altogether. Evidently, she and Todd had gotten into a tiff, because Pam overheard her mother begging him to come back. Pam never understood why Jeryca felt the way she felt about their mom until now. She cared more about a man than she did her own kids, and it made Pam feel that she was alone. She had Jeryca, but she was miles away, and that didn't help. She sighed as she heard her mother stomping down the hall, mumbling under her breath.

Pam shook her head, put her headphones on, and dozed off for a little while, but she was awakened by a hard shove.

"Get yo' ass up! Go clean up that living room and get that kitchen clean. All you do is lay your ass around here, trying to cause havoc in my life. You wanted my attention; now you got it! I hope you are happy. You ran Todd away, and he isn't coming back. If you had learned how to control your attitude, he'd still be here!"

Pam sat up with a confused look on her face. "I ran him away?"

"Yes, you did. You are just like Jeryca was at this age. She didn't want to see me happy either," Sheila grumbled.

Pam stood up and walked out of the room, heading into the kitchen with her mother close behind. "I don't know what you're talking about. Listen, I'm cleaning up like you asked me to. Now will you freaking back off?" Pam yelled, no longer able to hold her composure.

"Who the fuck are you yelling at? I will beat your ass up in here, girl. How dare you speak to me in that tone?" Sheila yelled as she advanced on Pam, getting face-to-face with her.

Pam shook her head and stepped backward, trying not to fight with her mother. "Mom, please! Like I would really fight with you! I'm doing what you asked me to do."

"I didn't think you would want any problems with me, although I should beat yo' ass for running Todd off anyway," Sheila spat out.

Pam didn't say a word. She took everything that her mother dished out until she was able to go back in her room, and even then, her mother was going in on her.

Pam finally drifted off to sleep after crying her eyes out. She couldn't imagine what had happened to make her mother hate her so much. She got up the early the next morning and left for school before her mother awoke. She walked down about a block and saw a black Jeep creeping up on her. She picked up her pace, glancing back here and there. The Jeep began to speed up, and she broke out into a run, but as she got to the corner, she realized that the Jeep was no longer behind her. She figured it must've turned down one of the side roads. She continued walking until she reached the bus stop, where there were a few other people waiting for the bus, and she felt a bit more secure.

Zack and Orlando were on a private jet to California. Sergio and Ramon needed them to pick up a shipment and to stand as lookout while Valerie, Desiree, and Smack, one of their new hit men, got rid of an old problem. Everyone stood to make over one hundred grand on the trip, except for Orlando. He owed Ramon and Sergio over $300,000, and until they gave him the word, everything he did for them was going to be pro bono.

"What's up, man?" Zack inquired, after noticing Orlando's quiet and timid behavior.

"Nothing. I'm just thinking 'bout Jeryca. That's all," he answered.

Orlando was thinking about Jeryca, but it wasn't what was bothering him. He could deal with the backlash from her, but he didn't know why they were going to California with some hitters. He hoped they weren't along on the ride to kill him, but if that was the case, Jeryca would also be dealt with. He wished he hadn't listened to Jeryca when she suggested that they spend the money and pay it back as more money was made. That girl was going to be the death of him, if she wasn't already. As he looked up and took in his surroundings, he noticed that everyone except for Zack was in their own world.

"I know she isn't tripping that you came on this run. Hell, that girl loves money, so she should be good," Zack replied.

"Jeryca trips if the sun is too bright, man. She will be okay," Orlando lied.

From Orlando's understanding, no one other than Desiree and Valerie was aware that he owed Ramon and Sergio money. Desiree was Ramon's chick, so she knew everything that was going on in the business. He was just going to relax and let whatever was going to happen, happen.

When they landed in California on a private strip, located on one of Ramon's ranches, they unloaded their cargo from the jet and into a black van. They were to take the cargo to a shipyard, where several of Ramon and Sergio's crooked police officers would meet them to trade off the guns for money.

The transaction moved smoothly, which calmed Orlando's nerves a bit. If they were going to take him out, what better opportunity than to let the cops kill him and classify it as a deal gone bad?

Later that evening, after all their business was finished, Orlando called to check on Jeryca. "Hey, what you doing?" he asked her once she picked up.

"Not working for free, I can guarantee you that," she replied angrily.

"Listen, I didn't call you to start that whole conversation over. I just wanted to check on you, and that's it," he replied.

Jeryca laughed. "Okay, Orlando. Well, I'm good. Thanks for calling and checking on me," she said before hanging up.

Orlando sat and looked at the phone for a few seconds before placing it back in his pocket. He shook his head and laughed. *Women!*

Jeryca slammed the phone down and screamed. How dare Orlando act as if she didn't have a right to be mad? With all the running that she and Orlando did for Ramon and Sergio, they owed them what they kept and then some, in her opinion. Somehow, she was going to make those two Colombian assholes pay for how they were treating them.

The following day, Orlando was back home and Jeryca was nowhere to be found. He called her phone. "Where you at?" he asked once she picked up.

"Does it matter where I am?" she answered.

"Girl, why are you playing with me? I'm tired and hungry. You haven't cooked or anything!" Orlando replied.

"You mean to tell me they make you work for free, *and* they starving your ass?" Jeryca became agitated.

"Jeryca, don't start that shit again. I'm not even going there with you. Just pick something up to eat while you are out and don't fucking take all day."

"Fine, I'll be home in a little while," Jeryca replied.

"Thank you," Orlando mumbled.

"Is there anything in particular you want?" she asked.

"Anything will do. I'm going to take me a bath and wait for you to get here," he replied, hanging up before she could respond.

Jeryca hung up and headed back toward the city. She wasn't expecting Orlando back so soon, and she had been heading to the spa located on the outskirts of town. "I guess my spa day will have to wait," she muttered to herself.

She turned the music up and drove to KFC to get Orlando a single meal. She wasn't hungry, and she wasn't cooking. She was still angry that Orlando stupidly agreed to make a few free runs. She felt that they could've offered him something for making the run.

Orlando wanted her to accept it, but Jeryca couldn't. She wanted the money. Jeryca wouldn't be happy until they agreed to pay him what they owed. If she had to call them herself, she would do just that. She wasn't going to let them make a fool out of Orlando. Yes, they may have owed Ramon and Sergio money, but dammit, if they didn't do what they did wouldn't no money be made. Orlando was their top moneymaker, and they needed to appreciate him for that and show it!

Chapter Fifteen

Dana called Detective Rone to see if Emily was in. She needed to go to her doctor's appointment, and they had been great getting her there when she had no other means of transportation. She hated being dependent on others, but it was something she had to deal with until she got better, which was her goal.

When Detective Rone answered the phone, his voice sounded strained.

"Uh, hello, Detective Rone. It's Dana Crisp. Is Emily there by chance?"

"No, she isn't here at the moment, but maybe I can help you," he replied.

"Well, I have an appointment today, but Brittany is busy, and Stephanie hasn't been here in a few days, and I can't miss this appointment," Dana answered.

"What time is your appointment, Dana?" he asked.

"It's at four o'clock," Dana answered.

"Let me check to see what my calendar looks like for today. Hold on."

Detective Rone looked over his calendar, but he already knew what his answer had to be. He agreed to pick Dana up, and he decided that it was time to reveal his true feelings for her. He didn't know how things were going to turn out, but he hoped she would still allow him to be a part of her life somehow after their talk. Her beauty astounded him from day one, but after getting to know her personally and studying her background, he knew he had to have her in his life.

A few days earlier, Detective Moore had cornered him and questioned him about his motives for helping Dana Crisp. He laughed at her and walked into his office, with her close on his heels.

"Rone," she had said, "I know you know that I'm not going to stop until I get to the bottom of this, so you need to talk to me."

"Talk to you about what? There isn't anything to tell. You asked me the other day for the Debra Fuller file and asked what happened with the investigation, and I will answer you once again. I followed up on that case, and after speaking with Ms. Fuller herself, I had no other option but to close the missing person case! So what are you saying that I should've done? Debra told me out of her own mouth that she was fine."

"I don't know, but because of your feelings for Dana, you dropped the ball somewhere, and this woman is now dead!" Detective Moore shouted as she slammed Debra's file on the table.

"My investigation was solid, and I did everything by the book! If you want to dig into it and prove otherwise, feel free to do so, but you better make sure you know what you're doing, and that's all I'm going to say," Detective Rone shouted.

Detective Moore had stood back, looked at him through squinted eyes, and shook her head. "No, there's something up with this, and I'm going to get to the bottom of it. Mark my words, Detective Rone, I will find out what you're trying to hide."

"Take this however you want to, and I mean every word I'm about to say: bitch, get the fuck out of my office. Now!" Detective Rone had growled. "When you stand in my face and accuse me of being partially responsible for an innocent woman's death, that's the most disrespectful thing you could do. I followed my job to the letter concerning the Debra Fuller case, and I won't let you or anyone else make me feel any different. Now, my personal life is just that,

Detective Moore, and I don't have to explain my actions regarding Dana Crisp or anyone else for that matter."

Detective Moore had leaned across his desk and smiled. "I'll be the bitch who brings in Dana Crisp and anyone else who was responsible for Debra Fuller's murder! Believe that!"

Dana waited patiently for Detective Rone to arrive. Brittany had gotten her dressed and cooked her breakfast before she left. Dana had time to reflect on her life and decided to place a long overdue call. She wasn't on the phone long, but when she hung up, she felt a bit more at ease. She couldn't continue to be a burden on her friends.

When Detective Rone came to the door, Dana smiled at him, but her smile soon faded as she saw the serious look on his face.

"Dana, how are you doing? Are you ready to go?"

"Yes, I'm ready. But what's wrong, Detective Rone?" she asked.

"Nothing. Well, Dana, I need to talk to you, but I just don't know where to start," he explained.

"Shit, start at the beginning," she replied.

She invited him in, and he closed the door behind him. He looked at her and then began filling her ears with a story that left Dana more confused than ever.

"Dana, I hope this won't change how you interact with me. I need you in my life, and I will do anything for you, sweetheart," he cried.

Dana sat emotionless. "Why did you wait 'til now to tell me your dirty little secret? I don't know how to take this. I knew you cared for me, but, Detective Rone, I'm speechless."

Detective Rone sat still for a moment then he stood up. "Come on, let's go, Dana."

As he wheeled Dana out of the house, he felt that he might have made a grave mistake by confiding in Dana. He wasn't going to lose her, though, no matter what he had to do.

Once he dropped her off, he called Brittany and asked her if she had dealt with their little problem yet.

"I'm dealing with it as we speak. Thank you for the heads-up. These guys you got over here helping me are on point."

"Just handle it. No thanks needed," he replied and hung up.

Brittany was with Rebecca and Officers Jay and Lewis in an old storage unit on the lot of the police yard where they kept all the older confiscated vehicles and property. Rone had informed her that he had found out that Rebecca was related to Brenda Gate, the woman Dana had shot during the robbery that took place in Thad's trap house. Rone had followed her all day until after she dropped Brenda off at her home

"Okay, let me ask you again: who are you, and why did you lie to me about who you were?" Brittany asked Rebecca, who was standing in front of her. Officers Jay and Lewis, out of uniform, were holding her by the arms while Brittany questioned her.

"I'm sure you already know the answers to those questions," Rebecca answered.

"Yes, I do, but I want to hear you say it, bitch!" Brittany yelled.

"Just get it over with! Rone don't want no mistakes," Jay said.

Brittany wanted to torture Rebecca, but they had to kill her and get out of the storage unit before the next officer made his rounds. She needed to know for herself why she was trying to hurt Dana but Detective Rone had found out himself when he roughed her up. She was Brenda's sister and Brenda, in fact, remembered what had happened to her and who did it.

Brenda saw and recognized Dana at the rehabilitation center her first time there. She overheard Brittany asking the therapist if he could refer any nurses who could take care of Dana, because she was having a hard time finding one. Brenda and Rebecca hatched a scheme where Rebecca would apply for the job and get in good with the girls, and then seek revenge on Dana for everything she did to Brenda.

"You know what, Rebecca? I can't say I blame you for wanting revenge for your sister. I mean, hell, I would've done the same thing. But you see, the way your luck's set up, sweetie, you shit out of it! You and your sister!"

As Rebecca began to speak, Brittany shook her head no and shot her with the .45 she had. After shooting her in the head three times, they wrapped her body up and stuck it in a trunk located in the building.

The three of them left the building as if nothing had transpired.

Once they were out of the police yard, Brittany thanked the two officers and walked to her car. She was ready to go and relax if she could. She couldn't believe that she had almost gotten her best friend killed. She had been so ready for a break that she accepted the first person who showed interest in the nursing position. From that point on she would do everything for Dana. No more outside people. She wouldn't trust anyone.

Chapter Sixteen

Tennessee

Zack was at the airport, making reservations to go meet Orlando for their next run for Sergio. He was also making Valerie's reservations. He saw a cute teddy bear in the gift shop window that he knew Valerie would love, so he went in to purchase it for her. When he walked out of the gift shop, he bumped into one of the most beautiful women he had ever met. He smiled at her and politely muttered, "Excuse me."

She didn't say a word at first, but looked at him curiously. Then, as reality set in, she blinked several times and smiled. "Sorry, but you have some attractive eyes. I almost lost myself," she said, grinning.

"I'm Zack, and you are?" he asked, as he extended his hand.

"I'm Rhonda," she replied, shaking his hand.

He held on to her hand and rubbed it with his thumb. "You have some very soft hands," he said and laughed.

"Thank you," she replied.

"I know this may sound a little forward, but do you have time for me to buy you a bite to eat? There are a lot of restaurants in the airport. I feel like I need to get to know you a bit more," he explained.

"Yes. I just need to make one phone call and let them know I'm here, but they can pick me up in an hour," she replied.

"Sounds good. I'll just wait over here while you make your call," Zack said.

Zack and Rhonda ate lunch while she explained that she was on a business trip and would only be in town for a few days. Zack told her that he had to leave town on a business trip himself, and wouldn't be back for a week or so.

She smiled at him. "I work for myself, so I can extend my trip if you really want to see me again," she teased.

"Hell yeah, I do. Your conversation is on point, and you're definitely fine as hell, so I would love to see you when I get back from this business trip," he replied.

They agreed that they would stay in touch by phone and meet the following weekend of his return.

After they parted ways, Zack turned his cell phone back on and read the three messages that Valerie had left for him because he'd kept her waiting so long. He smiled at her choice of words to describe him: asshole and wimp, among other foul words. Wouldn't she feel stupid when he walked in bearing gifts just because? And he was going to hold on to the receipt to prove to her that he was making the purchases way before she sent him the vile text messages.

As he walked to the car, he saw the lovely Rhonda getting into a car with a female and a guy, and he saw her pointing over at him and waving. The lady who was driving smiled, which told Zack that Rhonda had told them about their conversation.

As he drove off, he wondered what would happen between the two of them.

When Zack returned from the airport, the feeling that Rhonda left him with was too much to handle, so he turned to Valerie to calm the fire that burned within him.

"So, what is with these nasty text messages?" he asked, smiling and holding up his phone in one hand with his other hand behind his back.

"You know what was up! How dare you leave me here?"

Zack interrupted her rant by holding up the gift bag. "You were saying?" he asked jokingly.

Just like he expected she started going in on him, saying he couldn't play her like that by buying a gift after she texted him. He smiled and showed her the receipt that showed the time of purchase.

She started smiling. "Well, still, you left me here for a long time *papi!* Where you been?"

"I had to make a few calls and handle some business, but you were on my mind the entire time, sweetcakes!" he said as he walked up to her and took her in his arms. "Now where is the love?"

A few minutes later he had Valerie screaming to high heaven in pleasure. "Shit, Zack, fuck me, baby! Yes, just like that. You know how to please this pussy!" Valerie moaned as Zack was fucking her intensely.

He had her turned on her side with one of her legs thrown over his shoulder, and the other one stretched out to the far left. He liked Valerie, but she wasn't really what he wanted. She was a certified freak, and her pussy was grade A, but he just didn't feel real chemistry with her. Hell, she could snap his neck if she wanted to and he wasn't comfortable making a woman his main chick when she could strong-arm him.

Zack lay back after he came and he smoked a blunt. Valerie lay on his chest with her eyes closed. She said, "I've really enjoyed my time with you this week, but it seems like you have been preoccupied, baby."

"Yeah, I have been. I got to go down to Jamaica with Orlando to make this play, but I'm not feeling this trip," Zack explained.

"Well, hopefully, you will soon have enough cash where you don't have to do this anymore."

"It's not the runs I make that bother me. It's this particular run. Something isn't right," Zack explained.

"Don't go then, bae. You know you can tell them no," Valerie said.

"I can't leave my man hanging like that. I'm going to go, but just know I told you I wasn't feeling it."

Miami, Florida

"Hey, bae, why are you just sitting in here like this?" Jeryca asked.

"No reason. I just got off the phone with Ramon and Sergio, and they want me to make a quick play for them. I won't be getting paid for it, but I got to do it," Orlando answered.

"Hold up! What the fuck you mean you won't be getting paid for it? This is the second time you have had to do this! If you do the job, you get freaking paid!" Jeryca stormed.

"Yeah, but we owe them money, Jeryca. If I make this play for them, it will erase some of that debt from our plate," Orlando explained.

"I don't like that shit. That's why we need to be working for ourselves. We have been working our asses off for them, and they don't show any appreciation!" Jeryca fussed.

"We knew what we were getting into when we made this move, so don't start bitching about it now. We got to do what we got to do with your hot, spending ass!" Orlando snapped.

"So you're saying this is my fault?" Jeryca asked.

"I'm saying it's both our faults. We owe these men. I'm going to make this play for them, and that's the end of the conversation. I will be leaving in two days, and I will be back next week," Orlando stated in a way that told Jeryca the conversation was over.

Jeryca looked at him for a split second and then said, "Can I go with you?"

"No. This is something I'm going to be doing with Zack, and he will be here the day after tomorrow. I need you to help me pack a few bags and then ride with me to make a drop at the spot over on Fourth Avenue," he answered.

Jeryca didn't say a word. She went to the bedroom and pulled Orlando's suitcase out. She did as he asked, but she couldn't shake the feeling that Ramon and Sergio were playing them. They never moved anything for free, and they weren't going to use her like that. She was going to show Orlando that they could make all the same plays for themselves that they were making for Ramon and Sergio. She just had to devise a plan and make it work.

Two Days Later

After Jeryca dropped Orlando at the pier, she returned home and sat in the dining area, devising a plan to get Sergio and Ramon out of the way. She wanted power, and she aimed to have it. After attempting to call Valerie's number three times, she finally got up the nerve to let the call go through. She didn't get an answer, and she breathed a sigh of relief because she wasn't sure if she was doing the right thing, but a few seconds later, Valerie was calling her back.

"Here goes," she whispered to herself. "Hey, sis, how are you doing today?"

"I'm good, just sitting here looking at the newspaper. Shit, ain't too much I can do today. What you up to?"

"Nothing at all. Orlando had to go on a run for Ramon and Sergio, so I'm here by myself. Girl, get this: Orlando got to make the drop for free. We can't eat like that," Jeryca grumbled.

"Well, what else can you do?" Valerie asked.

"Shit, I'm hoping you can help me out or advise me on what I can do," Jeryca replied.

"How? Talk to me, sis."

"Well, I was thinking that maybe we could take over Ramon and Sergio's operation," Jeryca told her.

Valerie laughed. "Girl, have you lost your mind completely? You got to be crazy. I'ma act like I didn't hear that coming from you, 'cause I'd have to kill you if I thought you were serious. Girl, I think you need a plan B quick!"

Jeryca didn't say anything for a minute, but she realized that she might have just messed up. She played it off and started laughing also. "You know I was just joking. Shit, I said the same thing to Orlando, and he told me I was crazy. Y'all take things too serious."

"Yeah, well, I got to go. I got a call coming in on my other line. And, girl, please stop playing like that," Valerie said, laughing as she hung up.

Jeryca frowned as she hung up the phone and sat for a few minutes, contemplating her next move. If Valerie and Orlando wouldn't help her, then she would just have to find someone who would. She wasn't afraid of what Ramon and Sergio could do. Hell, she had dealt with Thad and his crew, and been involved in robberies, and she wasn't about to start allowing fear to get in her way of being rich.

When Valerie hung up from talking to Jeryca, she immediately called Desiree. She knew that Jeryca was probably just talking, but she wasn't going to trust her assumption just because she had formed somewhat of a friendship with her. Her loyalty remained with Ramon and Sergio.

"Hey, girl. What you got going on today?" Valerie asked when Desiree answered the phone.

"Shit, nothing right now, just been relaxing a bit," Desiree replied.

"Oh, okay. How you and yo' man getting along?" Valerie asked.

"We good, girl. That man is something else in bed. Say what you will about Ramon, but that man knows how to please me. His wife can't please him like I can," Desiree boasted.

Valerie began to laugh. "Girl, you are wild. Speaking of Ramon," she said, "um, I just got off the phone with Jeryca, and she was asking me if I wanted to help her take control of their empire."

"Take over whose empire?" Desiree asked, laughing.

"Ramon and Sergio's, girl. I haven't told Ramon yet. I called you first, 'cause I don't think she is serious at all, but you know I could just feel like that 'cause me and her are cool. What do you think?" Valerie asked.

"I think we should inform Ramon as soon as possible. We don't know what she is capable of, Valerie. I know you like her, but we've only known her for a li'l over a year. Ramon and Sergio we've known almost forever. Don't get caught up in the friendship zone with her."

"You right. But I know they are going to call a hit on her." Valerie sighed, and asked, "Who's making the call?"

"You can, 'cause she called you. They will wonder why you didn't call and it may be reason enough for them to question your loyalty," Desiree said.

"All right, I will call you later after I speak with them," Valerie replied.

Valerie hung up from talking with Desiree and immediately called Ramon. She explained to him what Jeryca had spoken to her about. She could hear the agitation in his voice as he asked her questions about their conversation. Valerie knew from the sound of his voice that Jeryca had made a grave mistake.

After she finished her call, she lay across her bed with her arm thrown across her face, wondering if she did the right thing. She really liked Jeryca and didn't want to see anything happen to her. She called Zack, hoping that he was available to talk. She needed to talk to someone so she could ease her mind. She dialed his number, and after the third ring, he picked up.

"Hey, babe. What's up?"

"Nothing much, boo, just wanted to hear your voice. Are you busy?" she asked him.

"Never too busy for you. How's your day going?"

"My day has been hectic, baby. I wish you were here so I could relieve the stress."

"Shit, me too. I miss you. When I get back from here, I want you and me to take a little vacation of our own. We can go to the beach, Hawaii, Paris, or anywhere else you want to go. Sound good to you?" he asked.

"Yes, it does. I think that's something we both will enjoy immensely. What you got on?" she asked.

"Girl, I can't do that right now. Give me about two hours and I got you." He laughed.

Valerie could hear Orlando in the background, laughing and teasing Zack about him blushing. Valerie started laughing. "Damn, bae, I'm sorry. I didn't know you were around anyone. Call me later when you are by yourself."

"All right, I got you."

Valerie felt a little better hearing Zack's voice. He always made her day better.

South America

Back in South America, Ramon and Sergio were devising a plan to rid themselves of what they now considered a huge problem. Over the past year, Jeryca and Orlando had been late on their payments for the third time, and now Jeryca was calling up one of their number-one top hitters to take them out. Valerie and Desiree were very loyal to them, and when they hesitantly revealed that Jeryca had gotten at them about a takeover, they knew it was time to make their presence felt. Jeryca thought that Valerie and Desiree would be loyal to her, but they were only loyal to the money. They had trusted Orlando with a lot of their product and hadn't yet seen over $300,000 at one time. They called up their most trusted cleaners and arranged a meeting.

"We have two problems to get rid of. Are you guys available to clean up?" Sergio asked the person on the other end.

As Sergio continued to talk, Ramon called up a few people himself. They were going to make an example out of Jeryca and Orlando, even though Orlando didn't have anything to do with her plan.

Orlando was going to die simply because he had brought a traitor in their midst. He should've been aware from the start of the type of person Jeryca was.

To kill them, they were going to send the very ones Jeryca trusted. Valerie and Desiree were more than willing to do the job, being that Ramon had set a $2 million price tag on both Jeryca's and Orlando's heads. However, Sergio was going to send some extra heat as a precaution, because the girls had become close to Jeryca and he wasn't going to give anyone a chance to shit on them.

They knew that Orlando and Zack were still in Jamaica handling some business for them. Ramon called down to his connects and told them to prolong the deal for two more days.

Jamaica

Once Orlando and Zack checked into their hotel they immediately received a call from their plug. "Meet us at the Hyatt." He gave them the address. "And make sure you bring the oil."

"Gotcha," Orlando replied, and hung up. "Let's go, man," he said, looking at Zack.

"Hell, we just got here! You mean to tell me a nigga can't relax?" he asked.

"I guess not, but the sooner we get this started the sooner we can go home!" Orlando replied.

"Man, damn! All right, let's go."

They arrived at the Hyatt within thirty minutes and sat at the back table and waited for their companion.

"This man ain't taking shit too serious if you ask me. He should've been here waiting for us. I hope this ain't no damn setup, man," Zack whined.

"Man, damn! Do you think Ramon would send us on this type of play knowing it's a setup?" Orlando replied.

"I don't put shit past nobody, man! All I know is if I was going to meet someone I'd have been here," Zack said nervously.

"Who is to say they aren't here watching us right now to make sure we legit? That's what I'd do if I was the one setting up a meeting like this," Orlando said.

"Yeah, well, I guess you may be right. Fuck, I just been feeling some kind of way about this particular trip," Zack admitted.

"Oh, Lord, don't jinx this shit!" Orlando frowned.

"Maybe that's him right there," Zack said, nodding to a man approaching them.

Indeed, it was him, but he didn't break stride. He motioned for Zack and Orlando to follow him. Orlando grabbed the sack he had, and they were led down a long stretch of stairs, into a cellar. There were three tables of card players and two empty tables. They were told to sit at one and place the bag on the other. Two women walked over and sat down at the table where the bag was and began counting the money. Another lady walked over to Orlando and Zack and asked if they would like a drink. Both guys said yes and placed their orders.

As they looked around, they noticed that almost everybody in the basement was strapped, even the ladies who were counting the money. They felt naked because they were instructed to leave their weapons at home. They played it cool while the ladies were counting.

After about fifteen minutes one of the women who was counting stood up and walked over to a man sitting at the bar and whispered something in his ear. He looked at the bartender and nodded. The bartender gave the woman a package, and she walked back over and sat down at the table with Orlando and Zack. Another man, who was playing cards, walked over and opened the bag that the woman was holding, and he counted out sixteen bricks of cocaine and two huge containers of heroin. Zack frowned and looked at Orlando but didn't say a word. They were led out of the cellar a different way from where they were led in, and still no one asked any questions.

Once they were alone back at the hotel, Zack yelled, "Man, what the fuck was that? I know they didn't send us all the way to Jamaica for this little, bitty-ass shit!"

"We have a few more tasks to fulfill while we are here, Zack," Orlando replied.

"Oh, yeah? And what the fuck are those tasks, Orlando? 'Cause, man, when I tell you I'm not feeling this, I mean I'm not feeling this!" Zack slammed his fist on the table hard, causing Orlando to jump a little bit.

"Man, calm the fuck down! I got this, bruh. Honest, I do. Ain't no shady shit going on, but in a few days, you will understand why we are here. Just relax and have a good vacation, my nigga. You got a free trip to Jamaica, so why complain?"

"Man, I'm going to sleep. I'm tired, and I need to rest," Zack replied.

"You aren't hungry?" Orlando asked.

Zack looked over at Orlando. "Hell naw! I'm sleepy."

"Shit. Whatever, dude! Don't get me wrong, but right now you sounding like a real bitch. You go on and go to sleep. I'ma call and let Jeryca know we made it okay," Orlando said.

"Yeah, whatever. Ay, who wears the britches: you or Jeryca, the way she got yo' ass checking in?" Zack yawned.

Orlando laughed. "Yeah, you tried that! Take yo' menopausing ass on to sleep, dude."

"Yeah, fuck you!" Zack laughed.

A few minutes later Zack was snoring, and Orlando was talking to Jeryca.

The next day Zack woke up fresh and ready to go. He took a shower and waited for Orlando to get dressed so that they could get their day started. They had four more pickups to make, and then they would wait for further instructions.

After the first two pickups, they were told to make the other two the next day. The guys were kind of relieved because they hadn't had any real time to check Jamaica out. Zack was ready to try one of the sexy women he was seeing every turn he took, and Orlando was just ready to relax. He wanted to try some real Jamaican cuisine. His first love was getting money; his second love was eating. He laughed as he wondered where Jeryca fitted in. "Somewhere in between." He laughed to himself.

When they returned to their rooms, after Zack had an unsuccessful day finding the right type of fuck, the telephone was ringing off the hook. They had several messages that they assumed were from Jeryca.

Zack answered the phone and barely said anything. Orlando knew at that point it had to be Ramon or Sergio.

After he hung up, Zack informed him, "Ay, I don't know what's going on, but Ramon just said he needs us to lie low for a few extra days."

"Man, I got other shit I need to do back home. I can't be down here like this," Orlando complained.

"The boss has spoken, man. We got to follow our instructions like you said yesterday. They may have heard something on their end, and it may not be good for us to return right now. Man, look, the work is almost finished, so let's relax for a few more days and enjoy some of this Jamaican pussy!" Zack joked, nudging Orlando.

Orlando smiled and walked to the door of their hotel room. "All right then, let's go check out some more of this wonderful scenery."

"You're not calling Jeryca to report in?" Zack asked.

"Nigga, bring yo' ass on! I see you got a lot of jokes," Orlando replied, walking out the door, laughing.

Zack stood up. "Ay, wait for me, damn!"

Chapter Seventeen

Over the last couple of days, Pam was struck with a feeling that she was being followed. The same black Jeep that she saw weeks back was now popping up everywhere she turned. She told Jeryca about it but was told that she was letting her imagination run wild. She didn't have any other people she could talk to, and she was feeling more alone than ever. Her mother had pushed her away, and her sister was too far away. She didn't want to go to Shirley's house, because she felt that she had been through more than enough with losing Farrah and raising Travis alone.

She wanted to believe that it was just her imagination as Jeryca had said, but the same guy seemed to pop up everywhere she went. She went to the grocery store, and he was there. She went to the mall, and he was there. He was everywhere, and it just didn't sit right in Pam's gut. She couldn't stay inside because her mom didn't want her there, so she would just have to pray that no one was after her. *I haven't done anything to anyone, and I'm a very friendly person.*

As Pam sighed and started walking from the park, a white van that she had seen before pulled up on her, and two guys jumped out, grabbed her, and threw her in the back. She screamed and kicked but to no avail. They handcuffed, blindfolded, and gagged her, and drove to a discreet location. Once the van came to a final stop, she heard the doors open and two male voices talking outside the van, before they dragged her out and took her inside. She was beyond frightened and had wet herself as a result.

She couldn't hear much of what was being said, but she didn't miss the mention of her sister's name.

Am I paying for something Jeryca did or didn't do? Is this Todd trying to force Jeryca to pay for his debt? Who the fuck has taken me, and why? she thought wildly.

She was frantic, and as she struggled in the chair she was in, it tilted over, and she hit the floor. The two men who held her hostage rushed in.

"Let's get her on the bed. We can't afford to have something happen to her," one of them said.

"All right, you get her hands, and I'll get her feet. Damn, she isn't heavy at all. I might be able to just pick her up myself, and you get the door for me," one of the men said.

Once they got her on the bed, her hands and legs were untied. Pam sat up, turning her head wildly until she felt them tug at the blindfold and remove the gag from her mouth.

Pam looked around the room, which only contained a bed, a radio, and a bucket. The windows were boarded up, and it stunk to high hell. She looked at her captors, who wore face masks and gloves. After hearing them say they had to keep her unharmed, and by the gentle way they handled her, she knew they weren't going to hurt her, so it eased her mind a bit.

"Get her a few jugs of water in here and some snacks. I'm going to place the call to let them know we set over here," the tall guy said.

As the two went about their tasks, Pam sat against the wall and wondered what type of karma she was reaping.

Miami, Florida
Tuesday evening, Jeryca and Orlando were sitting at Moore's Tavern, talking. They had decided to spend the day together with no in-

terruptions after Orlando returned from the six-day run he made for Ramon and Sergio. They picked Moore's Tavern because it was a very discreet bar located deep in the country. Jeryca was kind of out of her usual element. She wasn't as focused on Orlando as she normally would've been and Orlando knew something was wrong.

Jeryca had gotten Pam's message late the previous evening, and she decided that she was going to handle things personally. She hadn't told Orlando about the message, because she knew he would be ready to ride out immediately, but she was going to take care of it herself. She was more concerned about the man Pam said was following her than about Todd and her mother. She needed to look into that immediately. She was going to tell Orlando about everything when they returned home.

As they waited for the waitress, Orlando reached for Jeryca's hand. "Baby, is everything all right?"

"Yes, it is," she lied.

"Well, listen, we still owe Sergio and Ramon about three hundred thousand, and they aren't going to keep waiting for it. You got to control your spending habits. It's way out of control. I told you that before I went out of town. I return, and you have spent over twenty-five grand on fucking jewelry."

"My spending habit is not out of control. Baby, how is it that we bust our ass daily to make them their money, but we have a limit on what we can spend? That shit is crazy! You just came back from making a play for them! They are fucking greedy and I, for one, am not going to keep hustling for pennies! Fuck them! If you ask me, we can take them out of the equation," Jeryca leaned over and whispered harshly.

Orlando released Jeryca's hand and sat back, looking at Jeryca with his eyes squinted. "Are you serious? That has to be the craziest shit I've ever heard from anybody. Do you know that Ramon and Sergio can take us out with one phone call? They have killers working for them on almost every corner of the northern and southern continents. Take them out? You have lost your mind! You may not care about your life, but dammit, I love mine. We are making it just fine off our percentage. You just greedy as hell and want it all. It doesn't work that way, Jeryca."

"You know what, Orlando? I'm not going to waste my day talking about them. I want to just enjoy you," Jeryca murmured, as she slid her hand alongside his thigh.

"Okay, but we will finish this conversation, Jeryca," he said with a firm tone.

Jeryca turned her head slightly away from Orlando and then faced him with a forced smile. "Sure, just not now."

The two ate their dinner and went back to their condo. Jeryca had decided to talk to Orlando about the message that Pam had left, but then she decided that it could wait until morning. She had to get Orlando on board with her scheme to take over Sergio and Ramon's business. Orlando seemed to think it was farfetched, but she was in the mood to convince him that she was on the money.

When the two entered the condo, Orlando headed for the shower, and Jeryca watched him as he walked past her. She was always amazed at how solid his back and shoulders looked. He was toned and muscular, and she was happy that he was hers.

Jeryca walked into the bedroom, took off all her clothes, and walked into their open shower. She moved up to Orlando and started rubbing his back. She used the tip of her fingernails to scratch him lightly as she moved her hands up and down his spine and butt. Orlando leaned his head backward, enjoying the sensation she was giving him. She started kissing him lightly on his shoulder blade and then moved around to face him. She stood on her tiptoes and kissed him on his lips.

He grabbed her by her throat, pushed her back against the shower wall, and started sucking her breasts, taking time to enjoy each one of them. Jeryca moaned softly as she rubbed his head. She wanted him right then and there, and he was teasing her. She knew that Orlando knew that she wanted to fuck, but he wanted foreplay. He knew how to fuck with her head. He began licking and kissing her stomach. Orlando stood up, lifted up one of Jeryca's legs, positioned himself between them, and slid his dick up inside her. Jeryca gasped as he slowly moved in and out of her. Orlando started speeding up, but stopped quickly as he lifted Jeryca entirely up off the shower floor, still inside her, pressed her hard up against the shower wall again, and fucked Jeryca for five minutes straight roughhouse.

Jeryca loved it, but it took her a bit by surprise. Orlando had never been so dominant before. He was always gentle with her, but tonight was something new. Orlando placed Jeryca down, turned her around, and told her to place her palms up against the wall. When Jeryca was in position, Orlando slid inside her from behind and fucked her until he let out a loud groan that told Jeryca he had come. She was a bit disappointed, because he had always pleased her first, but this time, she was left unsatisfied and confused.

Once they showered, Jeryca went to bed, not noticing that her phone light was blinking, indicating she had a message. Orlando lay behind her and fell asleep. Jeryca wasn't going to let him get away with the half-ass performance he had just given her, and after an hour or so, she woke Orlando up by giving him a blowjob and riding him until she came. When Orlando went to sleep the second time, Jeryca was smiling and lying in his arms.

Memphis, Tennessee

Friday afternoon, Zack was at his home hanging from his bathroom shower rod. Three men and the beautiful young missy he had met a few days prior were sitting in his bathroom, asking him questions about Orlando and Jeryca. He wasn't a snitch, so they were going to have to kill him, which he knew was going to happen anyway. Rhonda, or whoever she was, had called him while he and Orlando were in Jamaica making their drop. She told him that she was going to be leaving soon and wanted to hang out with him.

They were supposed to have met up on that Saturday, but to his surprise, she had shown up on his doorstep early after he called to let her know that he was back in town. Being the man he was, he wasn't going to leave her standing outside. What Zack didn't know was that she had three goons on each side of the doorway, waiting to grab him.

As soon as he stepped to the side to let her in, the three men showed up out of nowhere, and one of them knocked him out cold. When he opened his eyes, he was hanging midair in his bathroom, and the girl was sitting in a chair, holding a gun, screwing on a silencer, and talking to one of the men. When they realized he was awake, that's when the interrogation began. They had cut him open, punched him repeatedly, and scalded him with hot water from the shower.

He didn't give them any information. Through his swollen eyes, he looked over at Rhonda and whispered to her, "Why are you doing this to me?"

The woman smiled. "You want to know why I am doing this?" she mockingly asked. "I will tell you exactly why I am. Do you remember Dana Crisp?" She could see from his expression that he recognized the name. "Well, you see, mother-fucker, Dana is my cousin, and I recognized your ass when I first saw you at the airport. I wasn't looking for you, but when I saw you, and I realized that you were checking me out, I went along with you. You see, I've heard so much about you and have seen so many pictures of you, I feel like I know you more than I know myself. Whether or not you tell me where Jeryca Mebane is, trust and believe I will find her and the rest of the bastards responsible for hurting Dana."

"Heard of me? Seen pictures of me? Who the hell are you?" Zack asked.

"Don't worry about who I am, nigga. Just know that I'm here to get revenge for Dana!" With those words, she shot Zack five times. As the blood from his body oozed down the drain, the woman and her brothers searched Zack's house thoroughly, until finally they found Zack's address book. One of the guys called Rhonda's attention to a small safe that he found in the closet behind a huge suitcase. It took two of them to carry it out and load it in the van.

When they got back to their hotel room, they opened it up and were shocked to find half a million dollars inside. They weren't looking for any money, so they considered it an added bonus. They split the money up and left Tennessee.

Jeryca and Orlando spent the weekend going over their finances. She wasn't happy about giving Ramon and Sergio half of their money, but Orlando insisted on giving it to them, and he wasn't going to be deterred from his decision. They had moved around close to $200,000 and decided to send it to Ramon first thing Monday morning.

Jeryca sulked for the entire weekend, refusing to talk to Orlando. Orlando, set in his own ways as well, was growing tired of Jeryca's greedy ways. He loved her, but he hated that side of her. He couldn't understand why she couldn't comprehend that Sergio and Ramon had given them the opportunity to live as comfortably as they were. He wasn't going to risk losing all he had gained, nor was he going to die behind Jeryca's greed. He'd hold her down for the right reasons, but he wasn't going to "ride or die" for bullshit. He would send her back to Brooklyn before he'd see her or him fucked up.

Monday morning Jeryca woke up, grabbed her phone to check what time it was, and noticed that she had a voicemail. Jeryca sat up and listened to a man telling her that they had her sister and that they were going to kill her if she didn't do as she was told. She gasped for breath as she listened to it repeatedly. Her hands began to shake, her breathing sped up, and she started hyperventilating.

Orlando sat up and jumped out of the bed, rushing to Jeryca's side. "Baby, calm down. Do I need to call 911? Baby, say something."

Orlando ran to the kitchen, grabbed a paper bag, and took it back to Jeryca. He placed it around her mouth and prompted her to calm down. He talked to her until her breathing was stable and she could talk.

"Someone . . . someone just . . ." She took a deep breath before continuing. "Someone just left me a voicemail and said they had my sister, and that they would kill her if I didn't do what they said. Oh, my God, someone took Pam!"

Brooklyn, New York

Sheila Mebane was up cooking breakfast when her phone started ringing. "Hello," she answered hurriedly.

"Mom, what is going on up there?" Jeryca asked.

"Nothing is going on up here. Why the hell you ask that?" Sheila asked.

"Where is Pam?" Jeryca asked, trying to calm her voice.

"I don't know. The little slut stayed out all night. It looks like she is following in her big sister's footsteps," she stated hatefully.

"Mom, why the hell haven't you been keeping a damn eye on Pam? You been so fucking busy chasing that boyfriend of yours that you forgot about Pam. If anything happens to her, it's your freaking fault! I bet you know where that lowlife is at!" Jeryca yelled into the receiver.

Sheila started laughing. "Nothing is going to happen to her hot ass. She may end up pregnant somewhere, but other than that Pam is okay. I really don't care what you or anyone else thinks about how I been acting, Jeryca. You are off somewhere living the good life while we are here struggling. So don't come at me about how I'm wrong."

"Is that right, Mother? Well, tell me why the fuck I just got a message telling me that my sister was kidnapped and they want money for her safe return! Tell me that!" Jeryca screamed into her cell phone.

Sheila sat on her bed speechless. She felt as if she couldn't breathe. Strangely enough, her concern wasn't for Pam. She was praying that Todd hadn't fucked up and kidnapped Pam, expecting Jeryca to pay out, because he was in for a rude awakening and would possibly end up in jail.

"Mother! Did you hear what I fucking said?"

"Yeah, I heard you," she answered, and hung up.

Jeryca sat wide-eyed on the couch, wondering who could've taken her sister. She was furious and wanted to kill somebody. She looked over at Orlando, who hadn't left her side since she received the phone call informing her that Pam had been snatched. Her mother had been so busy taking care of Todd's needs that she forgot about Pam. Jeryca knew what her mother was about for years, and she felt that she wasn't any better. She was so caught up in her own world that she wasn't there for her sister when she needed her to be. Jeryca dropped her head and began to cry.

Orlando hugged Jeryca and whispered, "Everything is going to be okay. We will get her back."

Jeryca shook her head, refusing to listen to Orlando, fearing the worst had already happened to her sister. She had done so many people wrong that it could be any number of people who wanted revenge.

Chapter Eighteen

Brittany was getting worried about Dana. It was going on two days since she had seen or heard from her. Brittany knew that Dana wasn't real close to her family and they were now residing in Connecticut. She called Dana's phone repeatedly and got no answer. From Brittany's understanding, Dana was supposed to have left for the rehabilitation center Monday in a taxi, and since that day, Dana hadn't been seen or heard from. Brittany also learned that Dana never made it to the center, so where was she? Brittany paced back and forth for hours, constantly looking out the door and window.

"Stephanie, have you heard from Dana?" she asked, once Stephanie walked into the house.

"No, I haven't. I'm not her keeper!" she answered.

Brittany stared at her as Stephanie walked past her, went into the bathroom, and closed the door. She was astonished at how Stephanie appeared to have not a care in the world about Dana's whereabouts, and she was starting to question if Stephanie had something to do with Dana's disappearance. *Where else could Dana be?* She was fighting to keep it together, because in her gut she felt that something wasn't right. The altercation that transpired between Stephanie and Dana a week back couldn't have been that serious to where Dana would just leave and not tell her where she was. She had called everywhere she could think of, looking for Dana.

When Stephanie walked out of the bathroom, Brittany turned and looked at her. "Listen, I know you got your own problems going on, but Dana has been missing for a few days, and I'm worried."

"First off, I don't have any problems. Everything is going just as I need it to. And second, Dana is a big girl and can handle her own. She doesn't need us following her as if we are her parents. Maybe that's why she left. Have you ever looked at it that way?" Stephanie asked.

"Listen, if Dana could walk, I'd agree with you, but she is in a freaking wheelchair, Stephanie!" Brittany yelled.

Stephanie sighed. "Well, have you called the police?"

"Not yet. I was waiting to see if you'd heard from her," Brittany said.

"Well, damn, you couldn't have been that worried!" Stephanie yelled, reaching for her cell phone. She dialed the one person she knew would care about Dana's disappearance. "Hey, Detective Rone, this is Stephanie. Have you by any chance heard from Dana?"

Brittany sat down on the couch as Stephanie talked with Detective Rone. She had been consumed with so much worry that she didn't think to call Detective Rone.

After Stephanie got off the phone, she looked at Stephanie. "He said the last time he saw her was when he dropped her off at the rehabilitation center last week. He said he'll send a few guys out to see if they can locate her, and he'll get back with us by tomorrow morning," Stephanie informed Brittany.

"Thanks." Brittany sat on the couch and started imagining all the worst scenarios possible that Dana could be faced with. Stephanie saw the worry in her face, and even though she was supposed to go back to Chris's house, she stayed with Brittany. She couldn't leave her there in the fragile state of mind she was in. The two women sat there and comforted each other until they fell asleep.

The following morning, Stephanie woke up and saw Brittany sitting on the couch with the phone in her hand. From the first time she laid eyes on Brittany, she assumed that something was up with her, but seeing how concerned she was about Dana, she knew that Dana had a true friend in her.

"Look, Brittany, I'm sure Dana is okay. Detective Rone is going to call any minute to tell us that he found her. Don't fret. You know our Dana is a fighter and won't let anybody hurt her," Stephanie said as she sat next to Brittany and hugged her.

The hug seemed to be Brittany's breaking point as tears began to roll down her cheeks. "Stephanie, all my life I've been a loner, and when I met Dana, she didn't hesitate to accept me for who I was. See, I've always been like a mother hen to the few people I did interact with, but they didn't like that part of me, so they eventually pulled away. Not Dana. She and I clicked from the very start, and I started to look upon her as my little sister. I would give her advice on lifestyle changes, and she accepted my positive criticism for what it was. She was so smart, and the way she grasped the law, I just knew she was the one to mentor. I could have talked her out of stealing from Thad from the beginning, but the money sounded good, and it was easy enough, so I fed into her plan and look where it has gotten her. I feel responsible for her being in this situation so, you see, that's why I do all the things I do for her. She is basically all I got."

Stephanie couldn't say a word. Brittany had never confided in her before, and to hear her say that Dana was all she had really sat in her spirit. She had known Dana for years and couldn't say that they had developed anything close to that kind of bond.

Finally finding her voice, Stephanie replied, "Dana will surface, I promise. I know you are worried, but everything is going to work out just fine. Come on, let's go eat some cereal. We got to have strength to beat Dana's ass when we see her for making us worry like this. Look at us over here."

"We can't beat Dana, Stephanie." Brittany laughed.

Well, we can at least pop her one." Stephanie laughed.

The two ladies ate their cereal and talked about what they were going to do when Dana got back. Stephanie even promised that she would try harder to get along with Dana.

After breakfast, both ladies posted up near the phone, anxiously awaiting Detective Rone's phone call. After two hours passed with no phone call from Detective Rone, the two ladies decided that they would go out and search on their own, but that brought no results either. Brittany was beginning to feel helpless all over again.

Chapter Nineteen

The day after Jeryca found out that Pam was kidnapped, she received a phone call telling her that she needed to head to Brooklyn, and if she wanted to see Pam alive again that she would have to do everything she was told. If they felt that she slipped in any way, Pam would die.

She put the phone on speaker so that Orlando could hear everything that was being said. After the call ended, Jeryca was lost in thought.

She didn't know what to think or say. She had been so thoughtless of Pam's needs, and now her sister was in a bad situation because of her. Pam had told her that she was being followed and she didn't listen. She should've sent for her as she promised her she would. However, she wasn't thinking about anyone other than herself. If she had all the money in the world, it couldn't fix her heart at that moment.

Pam had overheard what the guy had just said to Jeryca, and now her nerves were on edge.

Since the day that she was taken, the men had
been very kind to her. They fed her good food
and even played cards with her to make her feel
at ease. She was given plenty of water, and they
even allowed her to wash up in the room where
she was being kept. They didn't seem like the
kind of people who would harm her.

She hadn't felt afraid until that very moment.
She dropped her head and looked down at her
hands. Tears began to fall, and she couldn't stop
them. She lay down facing the wall and began to
pray that she wouldn't be murdered.

Ten minutes passed, and Pam was beginning
to get antsy. She wasn't going to just lie there as
if she didn't know that she could die. She sat up
on the edge of the bed and waited for the shorter
of the two guys who had taken her to walk into
the room. He set a sandwich down along with
some chips and a Sprite next to her bed. He
saw the frightened look on her face and reached
out to rub her hair, trying to reassure her that
everything was okay.

Pam took that moment to push at her captor,
and she ran down the hall. She didn't know
which way to go; all she knew was that she
needed to run and get away.

Her captor was quick on her heels, and before
she could get too far down the hall, he grabbed

her up and swung her around. Pam started screaming, which alerted the second man that something was wrong. He quickly entered the hallway and helped the other man drag her back into the room she was being held in.

The tall guy tossed her on the bed, but Pam bounced back up and attempted yet again to flee.

"Chill out or we are going to have to duct tape your mouth and tie you up! Is that what you want?" the shorter of the two asked.

"Please let me go! I promise I won't tell anyone anything. I don't deserve to be here!" she screamed.

"Listen, we don't call the shots, baby girl. We are just doing what we were told to do!" the shorter guy explained.

"Man, shut the fuck up! You ain't got to tell her shit. If we tell her to chill the fuck out, that's what she need to do or else I will strap her ass up! Now how about that!" the taller one said, facing Pam.

Pam was both angry and frightened, but she sat back on the bed with her back against the wall and her knees pulled up to her chest. She wasn't sure what else she could say. She told her captors that she wasn't going to be eating and that they could take the food away. Once she was closed up in the room alone, she started rocking back and forth, trying to come up with a new plan to escape. She wasn't going to allow them to hurt her without a good fight. She prayed that God would watch over her and guide her captors to have a change of heart.

As nighttime fell, Pam overheard her captors saying it was getting close to the time to move her. She didn't know what was going to happen, but she was preparing for the worst. She had to continue to be strong and pray that, somehow, she would come out of the situation all right.

Jeryca was filled with so many emotions trying to figure out who could've been responsible for kidnapping Pam as they rode up the highway, heading to Brooklyn. She never thought she'd ever see the sight of that city again, especially not for the reason she was going for. She had left a trail of unresolved issues back there, and she didn't have the time or the energy to deal with them, so she was going to keep a very low profile until the kidnappers told her where to drop the money off and where she could find her sister. She prayed that she found Pam alive.

Orlando couldn't believe his luck. Of all the women to fall in love with, he had to fall in love with Jeryca, a greedy, conniving, and selfish woman. She would do anything to keep from returning Ramon and Sergio's money to them. He just hoped that this wasn't a ploy to stash more money. If it was, he would kill her himself.

They were traveling in the dead of night and were going to arrive early in the morning. They were instructed to check in at the West End Hotel, and once there, to contact them from that hotel's phone.

Jeryca and Orlando checked into the designated hotel, and after getting into the room reserved for them, Jeryca immediately called the number her sister's captors had given them. "This is Jeryca. We are here. What do you want us to do next?"

"We will call to your room with further instructions in a few hours. Do you have the money?"

"Can I please speak to Pam?" Jeryca asked, ignoring the kidnapper's question.

"In time you will be with Pam, but right now, I need to know if you got the fucking money!"

"I want to know if my sister is okay! I'm not giving up a dime until I speak to my sister!" Jeryca yelled as she gripped the phone tightly. Her hands were shaking, and tears filled her eyes. Orlando knew in that moment that Jeryca couldn't have set the kidnapping up. If she had, she was one hell of an actress.

"Jeryca, give me the phone. I'll handle this," Orlando ordered.

"No! I want to speak to my sister now! Fucking cowards couldn't deal with me, so they pick on a young teenage girl to get to me. Fuck them! Let me speak to Pam now!" she screamed.

Orlando rushed forward and grabbed the phone from Jeryca. She started yelling and hitting him, angry that he wouldn't let her talk to the kidnappers. Orlando ducked and dodged Jeryca's fists the best he could as he concluded the phone call, assuring the kidnappers that they had the money. Once Orlando was off the phone, he turned and looked at Jeryca long and hard, while she looked at him as if he were a stranger.

"Why did you do that? You told them we had the money before they let us speak to Pam! How do we know she is alive?" Jeryca sobbed.

"They said Pam would be there when we get there, and that they would let her go before we give them the cash."

"They could be lying!" she cried.

"You're right, but we have no other options. We could've had Sergio and Ramon help us, but after that stunt you pulled with Valerie, we will be lucky if they don't come after us. That is if we survive this," Orlando murmured.

Jeryca dropped her head and sighed. "I really fucked things up with my life and may have even caused the death of my sister. I will die a thousand times over if they don't let Pam go." Jeryca began to cry as she rested in Orlando's arms until she fell asleep.

Jeryca woke up and found that Orlando was gone. She decided that she wasn't going to chance anything happening to her sister. She was going to make the ultimate sacrifice: her freedom for her sister's life. She also had to make sure that Pam would be in a better place when and if she was found. There was no way that she was going to give up her life only to have Pam in the same situation with Sheila. She called the only person she knew would help Pam.

"Hey, Shirley, how are you? This is Jeryca."

"Oh, my God! Jeryca, baby, it's been a long time. How are you doing?" Shirley asked.

"Not too good, ma. I will explain everything to you in a little while, but I want to know if Pam can stay with you until she is capable of doing for herself. I have a few dollars stashed away, and a nice house located in Miami that I will sign over to you today, if you can help," Pam told her sadly.

"Jeryca, what's wrong?" Shirley asked.

"I can't go into detail yet. I just need to know if you can help her out," Jeryca inquired again.

"Of course I will help her. You know I will," Shirley answered.

"Thanks, ma, you are the best. Look, I got to make a few more calls and run a few errands, but I will contact you later on, okay?" Jeryca said, before hanging up.

Jeryca called the police station and asked to speak to Detective Rone. He didn't answer, so she left him a brief message. "Detective Rone, guess who this is. It's Jeryca Mebane. I know you been looking for me for torching Dana Crisp, and I am willing to turn myself in, plus give you all the information you need to build a case against Dana Crisp and Brittany Howell. However, I need you to help me with a big problem that I find myself faced with. Please call me as soon as possible." She left her phone number and hung up.

Eavesdropping on the message, Detective Moore smiled and wrote down Jeryca's information. She wasn't going to allow Detective Rone to botch another case against Dana Crisp. After she got into her office, she sat down at her desk and dialed Jeryca's number.

She introduced herself as Detective Moore and explained that she was handling a few of

Rone's cases, as he was swamped with other cases.

Jeryca wasn't quite sure if she should talk to the detective, but she couldn't waste time trying to figure out if the woman was on the up-and-up. She explained everything to Detective Moore. They agreed to meet and discuss everything in person. Jeryca's better judgment was telling her not to do it, but she had to do something, and if she had to give up everything for her sister, she would.

After getting off the phone with the detective, Jeryca made one last phone call to her attorney in Miami. She asked him to draw up ownership transfer papers to her condo, and to do a title change for her car. The condo and one of the cars were in her name, and she was going to give it all to Shirley and Pam, to make sure they were secure. She also had $250,000 transferred into an account for Shirley and a hundred grand transferred into an account for Pam. It came from her personal nest egg that she had been saving up for months.

The $300,000 Orlando was gathering to pay Pam's ransom would never make it to the kidnappers' hands, if Jeryca could help it.

After meeting with Detective Moore, Jeryca felt somewhat relieved. She hadn't given Detective

Moore all the info on Dana Crisp, but she promised she would if they helped her save her sister. She wrote a very detailed letter, explaining everything that had transpired and who played what part and gave descriptive information about Debra's death. The only one of the girls who wasn't implicated in anything was Stephanie. Jeryca decided that enough backstabbing and snitching had occurred between them, and the only reason she was snitching on Dana was because of Farrah. She wasn't going to let her get away with that. She just hoped that Farrah was at peace, and would forgive her for the part she played in the entire mess. Jeryca realized that since the day they devised the plan to rob Thad and gain a wealth that wasn't theirs, nothing but bad things had happened to them and the ones they loved.

The following day, Jeryca was notified that the time for the drop had changed, and she was advised that if they brought the police Pam was dead. Once all the changes were discussed, Jeryca immediately got off the phone and called Detective Moore. She still hadn't told Orlando about the deal she had made with the detective.

Detective Moore wasn't in at the time, so Jeryca left her a message, telling her about all the changes. She knew that Detective Moore had placed a tracker on her rental, and would be able to find them easily.

As the time neared to go and make the drop, Jeryca was beginning to feel uneasiness. Detective Moore hadn't called her back as of yet, and she didn't want to walk into a bad situation.

Orlando walked into the room where Jeryca was sitting. "Come on, bae, we got to get a move on. They told us not to be late."

Jeryca sighed and nodded. She wasn't sure what she was about to walk into, but she was as ready as she would ever be. They checked out of the hotel, got into their rental, and headed down the interstate. They jumped off at exit 321 and turned on Fairway Road. They followed the instructions to the letter and found their destination with no problem.

As they entered the location, Jeryca heard a rumbling sound from behind her.

"Bae, watch—" said Orlando.

Before she could utter one word, she and Orlando were both knocked unconscious. When she came to it was like déjà vu. She and Orlando were tied to some chairs, and there were two masked men standing in front of them with shotguns.

Chapter Twenty

"Hey, Brittany, how are you doing?" Dana asked quietly when Brittany picked up the phone.

"Dana! Where the hell have you been?" Brittany yelled, causing Stephanie to look at her curiously.

"That doesn't matter. Can you and Stephanie meet me at the Lakeshore address, please? I have something I need to talk to you about. I have decided to deal with my situation on my own, and I really hope you will understand. I hate being a burden on anyone and after hearing that Detective Rone is my father—"

"Detective Rone is what?" Brittany yelled.

"Yes. He told me that, from the first time he saw me, he knew there was something familiar about me. At first, he thought he was attracted to me in a romantic way, but he soon learned that I was his daughter. He met my mom years before I was born, but they couldn't seem to get along, and after he left for college, my mother seemed to have disappeared. He asked if he could be a part of my life now and get to know me as a father should, so I agreed, and I have been staying at his home, doing just that. However, the time away allowed me to focus on my situation more, and I decided that I have to start doing things on my own, so I did just that."

"Wait a minute, Dana, we called Detective Rone, and he told us he hadn't seen you. We were worried like crazy," Brittany stated.

"I told him not to tell anyone where I was until I told him it was okay," Dana answered.

"Wow, Dana, that's crazy. How are you feeling?" Brittany asked.

"I'm good now, thanks. However, I would really like it if you all could meet me around seven this evening. I had put a few things in motion a few weeks ago, and I need to let you and Steph in on it," Dana replied.

"Yes, we can do that," Brittany agreed.

"Thanks. I got to go, and I will see you soon," Dana replied.

As Dana was wheeled into the abandoned house on Lakeshore Drive, she could hear Jeryca telling Brittany that she wasn't afraid of none of them, and if they hurt one hair on Pam's head, she was going to make sure they paid dearly.

"I don't know what the hell you are talking about! Who the fuck took Pam?" Brittany asked.

She also heard Brittany asking Stephanie where Dana was. "I don't know, Brittany, but she should've been here by now," Stephanie answered.

As Dana was rolled into the back den area where everyone was waiting for her, she heard Brittany and Stephanie muttering, "What the fuck?"

Thad stood behind Dana, smiling. He placed his hand on her shoulder and looked at Stephanie and Brittany. "We have called a truce for this occasion. Don't worry. You can go back to hating me tomorrow, but tonight, I got a personal score to settle with Orlando here. You see, Orlando, I know that you and this bitch were responsible for my brother's death, and you will both pay dearly with your lives. Chris, bring Pam in here now!" Thad ordered.

"Man, are you seriously going to do this?" Chris asked.

"Nigga, just go do what I fucking said," Thad ordered angrily.

"I will go with him and help him bring her in here," Stephanie said, as she glanced at Chris.

As the two left to get Pam, Dana asked to be wheeled over so that she could sit face-to-face with Jeryca. She wanted to see the expression on Jeryca's face when she saw what the fire had done. Thad pushed Dana in front of Jeryca, still tied to her seat next to Orlando. Orlando looked over at Thad, as he stood next to Jeryca with hatred in his eyes.

"What's that look supposed to mean, nigga? You don't scare me at all. Never have. You got my brother killed, and now it's your turn to watch someone you love die."

"What do you mean, 'watch someone I love die'?" Orlando asked.

"Shit, I know you ain't no fool. You know exactly what I mean! I see how much you love Jeryca, and she loves you as well. Hell, that bitch showered you with loyalty and respect by shitting on me. I put her in the position to be who she is now, and she stabbed me and everyone here in the back. Man, look at what she did to Dana!" Thad said calmly.

"Dana, what are you doing with Thad and what is going on with Pam?" Brittany asked agitatedly.

"Shit, I ran into Thad a few weeks back when I went to visit Travis and Shirley. She called me and said that he had been asking for me. When we got there, Thad and Chris were there. We didn't talk at first, but after running into him a second time, I decided to confront him on a few things. Once we talked, we realized we had a few problems in common to take care of," Dana explained.

"Who is 'we'?" Brittany asked.

"The first time I met with Thad, I was with Stephanie. I had an appointment, and Stephanie sat with me for a little while, but then she explained that she had to make a quick run. When she didn't come right back, I called my cousin to pick me up," Dana said.

"Who is your cousin?" Brittany asked.

Dana looked at Brittany and smiled. "Emily is my cousin. Detective Emily Jackson."

Everyone stood quiet for a minute, and then a voice came from the doorway. "Yeah, I am Dana's cousin, and when I learned that someone had tried to kill her, I asked to be on the case. No one knew that Dana was my cousin, so I was allowed to work on it, and I worked hard to track this bitch down. When I went to my sister's wedding in Tennessee, I saw Zack's ass, and I knew it was my chance to get the information I needed to find Jeryca. I got my brothers to scoop his ass up, and after we got Jeryca and Orlando's location, we devised this plan to kidnap Pam and get Jeryca's ass back here so Dana could repay her for what she did to her. The day I picked Dana up from her appointment, we went to the bar and who was there, asking Dana a thousand and one questions about Keith? Yep, you got it, good ol' Thad here. Dana refused to talk to him at first, but I pulled up on him the next day to make sure he wasn't trying to hurt my cousin. I convinced her to at least hear him out, and I assured her that if he was up to anything, I would be there to protect her. The two of them finally talked and found out they both had an itch to scratch with these two. Oh, and Chris was very helpful to us in kidnapping Pam," Emily confessed.

"But, Dana, why didn't you let us in on it?" Brittany asked.

"I knew the bills were eating your pockets up and you had so much on your mind, I didn't want to burden you with any of this. Britt, I appreciate everything you do for me, but I needed to do this for me," Dana explained.

Orlando sat quietly, listening to Emily talk until Brittany interrupted them. "Why the hell haven't Chris and Stephanie gotten back yet?"

Dana looked around toward Brittany and Jeryca and started laughing. "Well, it looks like you might have a problem on your hands. Bitch, you will never touch my sister with them deformed hands of yours! I guess you thought I was going to feel sorry for what I did but I'm not. You can kill—"

Before she could finish her statement, Dana rammed her knife in Jeryca's gut. She smiled at Jeryca as she twisted the knife to the left and right, looking Jeryca in her eyes as the life slipped slowly from her. Blood started dripping from her mouth as she moaned and coughed. Dana smiled and drove the knife deeper into her gut until Jeryca was silent.

Orlando yelled and fought against the ropes that held him in his chair. He began to scream once he realized that Jeryca was dead. Thad smiled. "Don't worry, brother, you will soon join her." He pulled out a .45 revolver and shot Orlando in the head.

Just then, Detective Moore and the task squad rushed into the abandoned house with their guns drawn, screaming that they were in the house. Upon entering the front room, they saw Thad standing over Orlando's dead body, with a gun pointed downward.

"Drop the gun now! Do what we said. Drop the gun and get on the floor!" Detective Moore yelled.

Thad began to smile. He had lost the only person who meant anything to him: his brother, Toby. Sergio was after him, and almost all his money had been spent. Thad decided that he wasn't going to sit behind bars waiting for a death sentence. As he turned to face Detective Moore, he lifted the gun, and before he could spin completely around, the officers opened fire on him. He died instantly.

Dana, Brittany, and Emily were arrested and placed in separate police cars. Before they were taken out of the house, Dana watched the officers go to Jeryca's body, and she felt a moment of satisfaction. She had gotten her revenge on the person responsible for her now-gross appearance. She smiled all the way to her police car.

Brittany sat in the back of her police car angry and disappointed. She never imagined that she would be in need of legal representation. However, she knew deep down that they were going to catch up with her sooner or later. As she glanced over to where Dana was, she was shocked to see that she was smiling. Brittany shook her head. "That bitch is crazy!" she said to herself.

Emily Jackson held her head down as she contemplated suicide herself. She knew deep down that Jeryca deserved to die, but she couldn't believe that Detective Moore found them that quick. Someone had to have dimed them out, but who? She cringed at the sight of Pam Mebane being wheeled out the house on a stretcher. The police had found her in the basement of the abandoned house. She knew that Pam would be affected for the rest of her life by what they did, and for that alone, Emily felt remorse.

Stephanie and Chris rode down 85-South heading toward Atlanta, Georgia. She smiled as she glanced over at Chris, who was counting a wad of money.

"Girl, you used your head on that power move. They never knew what was happening." Chris laughed.

"They all got what they deserved. They were murderers and needed to pay for their crime. I wish I could've seen the look on Brittany's face when the police busted in the house," Stephanie replied.

"Girl, I knew you were a trap queen. I love you. I honestly do. After I bumped into you at the mall, I didn't think you were ever going to speak to me again. Then when you called me and suggested we work together to remove ourselves from the grasp of Thad and Dana, I was more than willing. I know I did you wrong and God knows I regretted every day how I treated you," Chris explained.

As Stephanie turned off at exit 240, Chris looked at her oddly. Stephanie glanced over at him and laughed. "Why are you looking at me like that? Look at the gas hand. We need to gas up before we're sitting on the side of the road."

When they pulled into the service station beside the gas pump, Stephanie got out and leaned back into the car. "Do you want a drink or something?"

Chris leaned his head back against the head-rest and shook his head. He looked content and happy. Stephanie shut the door and walked into the store to pay for the gas. She walked slowly down the aisle looking at the chips and grabbed a bag of spicy Doritos and two Sprites. She placed the items on the counter. "Do you have a restroom I can use?"

"Yes, it's located at the back to the right," the cashier said, pointing.

After Stephanie paid for her items and used the bathroom, she placed the items in her car and pumped her gas. She got back into the car and looked over at Chris. His eyes were closed, and his head was tilted to the side. Stephanie smiled and pulled off. Five minutes later as she was pulling back onto the ramp, she heard a noise in the seat behind her.

She stopped quickly and glanced behind her, and out from the darkness, Deondre popped up.

"Damn, bae, don't scare me like that! You could've given me a signal that you were in here!" Stephanie yelled, holding her chest.

"My fault, girl! Calm down." Deondre laughed.

"So it's done?" Stephanie asked, glancing at Chris's still body.

"Yeah, I choked his ass out! I think his neck broke, 'cause I felt something pop. Come on, drive down to the exit and we will toss his ass out near the river," Deondre said as he sat back and lit a blunt. "Damn, this nigga got that fire!" he said, coughing and holding the blunt up that he took from Chris after he killed him.

Stephanie smiled as she drove down the interstate. After they threw Chris's body into the river, she and Deondre drove off and headed back up to Connecticut. They had a small apartment that Deondre had found for them a few weeks earlier.

Stephanie was happy to be out from under Dana's and Brittany's thumbs. She couldn't believe that Dana would've stooped so low for revenge that she was willing to kill a child. She was going to check on Pam at a later date, but at that moment she was going to be content with finally being on her own.

After Dana's arrest, Detective Rone was investigated and subsequently fired, then brought up on charges himself. He was charged with mis-handling evidence and received seven years' probation for his part in the cover-up. Detective Rone still had connections in the Bureau, and he was going to contact them as soon as he could. Maybe if he pulled enough strings, he could get Dana and her girls out of the fix they were in. Besides, he had covered up a lot more than just his own discretions. A few people inside and out of the force owed him a few favors, and he was going to call on them.

Brittany was a better attorney than she was a defendant. After only an hour of interrogation, she confessed to the murder of Debra Fuller. Although she didn't snitch on Dana or Minx, the detectives found enough evidence against them to charge them as well. Deondre was never considered a suspect.

Dana and Brittany each were facing twenty years in prison for the murder of Jeryca Mebane. Even though Dana was the one who actually killed Jeryca, Brittany was an accessory to it and was looking at the same sentence as Dana. Dana didn't know how she was going to get herself out of her current fix, but she had to do something. As she sat back in her cell, her brain started pushing at a thousand miles per hour.

Emily was the only one who was facing two lessor charges of kidnapping and obstructing and delaying an officer. She was of course stripped of her title and was just a regular civilian like everyone else, although she was given special treatment.

She called Rone one day to ask about Dana. "Hey, Rone."

"Hey, how are you doing, Emily? Are they at least treating you okay?" he asked.

"Yes, sir. Have you heard from Dana? I haven't heard a peep from her in a day or so. She has been stuck in her cell. We are kind of worried about her," she explained.

"No, but I will see if I can get someone I trust to go check on her. You know how that goes."

"Yes, I do. Well, I'm not gonna hold you any longer. I just wanted to give you the scoop on your daughter."

"Emily, I do thank you for keeping my secret until I was able to tell her," Rone said.

He sat back on his couch and wondered what was going on with Dana. He knew that she was a loner mostly on the outside, but he couldn't imagine what she was doing or why she wasn't going out of her cell in jail. He was told that she had a roommate and the roommate was into the Bible. He needed to get his daughter out of that hellhole and quickly. He racked his brain trying to formulate a plan, and after a few hours he finally came up with one. He immediately placed a few calls, requesting more favors that were owed to him.

"Emily Jackson! You have a visitor," one of the guards yelled in her cell.

She got up and got ready, and when she was ready, the guard took her down to visitation. There, she was greeted by an attorney.

"Hello, my name is Mr. Ford, and Mr. Rone hired me to represent you. How are you doing, Ms. Jackson?"

"I'm as good as can be expected in this place," she replied.

"Yeah, well, I guess it's a lot different being on the other side of the law," Ford stated.

Emily frowned but didn't say a word.

"I have a few documents for you to sign, and if these guards give you any trouble about taking this back with you let me know. You are a detective—well, you were—so you know that what we say is privileged. Those documents are privileged as well," he explained.

They talked for a few minutes and then Emily looked over the paperwork. She quickly looked at him. "Is this for real?"

"As real as it gets!" He smiled.

"Are you sure this is the route we need to take?" she asked.

"Is that not a good deal?" he asked.

"It's the best thing I've heard since I got in this mess," she replied.

"Well, all right. So it's a go?" he asked.

"Hell yeah, it is! Thank you so much!" She smiled.

"Just doing my job, ma'am."

They ended their conversation, and Emily was escorted back to her cell. She prayed that everything she read in those documents went smoothly.

Later, Emily walked into Dana's cell and saw her crumbled on the floor. She was unresponsive and barely breathing. She ran out of the cell screaming for help.

Two of the guards raced over to see what was going on and immediately called for the paramedics. Emily stood back with tears in her eyes. As they were bringing her out, they were doing CPR on her. In the distance, she heard a scream echo throughout the cellblock. Brittany had caught sight of her friend being taken out on a stretcher. It took several guards to contain her while the area was cleared for Dana.

Once they put her in the ambulance, they called ahead to the hospital to inform them that they had a young female Dana Crisp arriving DOA!

Brittany was placed in her cell, and Emily was stuck in shock of everything. She sat with her mouth agape, speechless. The good news she had gotten earlier meant nothing to her now. She had learned that she was going to go before the judge, and because of misplaced evidence, she would be released on multiple technicalities.

An hour later they were given the news that Dana had died. Emily's joy of going home was short-lived as she mourned her favorite cousin.

Brittany had heard the news and flipped out. She had to be sedated, and later that week she was sent to a mental health hospital. She had stopped eating, talking, and bathing. She simply gave up on life.

A few days later, Emily went in front of the judge, and after reprimanding her, the judge had no other choice but to release her. It seemed that all the evidence against them had been lost. Brittany could've gotten off as well, but she had sealed her fate by confessing to a murder that had nothing to do with the fire.

When Emily left the jail, she was picked up by Rone. They rode in silence for about a mile before she spoke. "How are you doing?"

"I'm okay, I guess," he replied.

"So what have you been doing with yourself?" she asked.

"Just trying to keep my head above water. I never imagined my life would turn out like this," he admitted.

"Me either. I'm not sure where you can drop me off. I have nowhere to go."

He smiled sadly. "I'm going to leave town tomorrow. There isn't anything else keeping me here."

"That sounds like a great idea. Oh, and thank you for helping me get out," she said.

"My plan was to get all of you out. I had no idea that Brittany had pled guilty to murdering Debra, but I guess things happen for a reason."

"Yeah, I guess."

There was about twenty minutes of silence as they drove. Then she asked, "So where are we going?"

"Thought I'd say my final good-byes to Dana. You know, it's bittersweet."

"What is?" Emily asked.

"How we end up together to do one last check on Dana."

Emily didn't say a word. After riding about two and a half miles into another state, Rone turned down a long driveway. He parked his car in the garage of a house.

"I thought we were going to say good-bye to Dana," Emily said.

"We are," he replied.

They walked into the house toward a back room. She frowned as she followed Rone into the room. What she saw froze her in her footsteps.

"Well, hell, don't just stand there. Come and give me a hug!"

"Dana!" Emily cried. "But how?" she asked, searching her face.

Rone said, "Well, I had a friend of mine mix up a li'l something and put it in Dana's food to make it appear that she was going into cardiac arrest. One of the paramedics who answered the call was Ted. He made sure that they were in close proximity to the jail and when the call was dispatched they answered. Dana arrived at the hospital, and my two guys were waiting for her. They took her to a hospital room where the chaplain identified the body and signed paperwork. Bodies were switched, and she was brought here afterward. I wasn't able to get her off on a technicality. I couldn't let them send her away for good. We are leaving in the morning, and you can come with us if you like."

"I'm definitely coming with."

The following morning they boarded a private plane and flew to Hawaii.

Pam was released a few days later from the hospital into Shirley's care. They had a small funeral with only a few family members and friends present. Jeryca was cremated, and Pam was given her ashes. After receiving instructions from Jeryca before she was killed, Shirley packed up all their belongings and moved to the condo that Jeryca and Orlando had shared. Jeryca had left a package in the condo that included the deed to the condo and a will that left Pam over $175,000 and two cars.

Jeryca had also left a bundle of cash in her back bedroom that belonged to her. Pam found it as she rummaged through what she knew was Jeryca's closet. It was in a huge manila folder with Pam's name on it. There was a little over a hundred thousand dollars in it. Two letters were also enclosed: one addressed to Shirley and the other to Pam. Pam opened her letter immediately.

Hey, li'l sister, if you got your hands on this letter I know that you been nosing around in my room, but most importantly, you are okay! I regret so much in my life, li'l sis, and not being there for you is my greatest regret. Baby girl, I had no doubt in my mind that you were all right when those kidnappers called me because my heart was still beating. We have a connection, and I can feel it when you are hurt no matter how far apart we are.

I also know that whoever had you was setting up a trap to get me, and knowing that, I'm guessing that I'm probably dead. You know in life, when you do so many awful things, sooner or later you try to right a few of your wrongs. A few of my regrets rest where you are.

I called Shirley the day after I arrived in Brooklyn and asked her to take care of you in the event that I was killed. You see, I never told you about my childhood, but I can tell you that I do know what it's like to live with Mom when she is involved with a no-good man. Shirley knows a lot about what happened and one day I want you to sit down and ask her to tell you my story.

You know I love you, sis, and that is the only thing as of late that I will never

*regret doing. You got to hold it down for
me, baby girl, okay? I love you, I love you,
I love you! Never ever forget that.*

Pam read her letter repeatedly. She smiled as
tears streamed down her face. She was going to
miss her sister very much, and she felt an empty
space inside her. It suddenly hit her hard as the
painful reality set in that her sister was gone
forever and that she went to Brooklyn to save
her knowing she would most likely die.

Pam dropped to her knees and started pleading with God to forgive her sister's wrongdoings
and allow her entrance in heaven. As soon as she
finished praying, she looked up and saw Travis
standing in front of her.

"Are you okay, Pammy?" he asked.

"Yes, I am, little man. Come here." She sat
back against the bed and placed Travis in her
arms. She leaned back and closed her eyes while
holding on to Travis tightly. And from out of
nowhere, she started singing a verse from the
Whitney Houston version of "I Will Always Love
You":

I hope life treats you kind
And I hope you have all you've dreamed
of
And I wish you joy and happiness
But above all this, I wish you love

As she started in on the verse, she dropped her head against Travis's head and began to cry. He turned around and wrapped his arms around her and cried right along with her.

Shirley walked in and was stuck in the doorway watching the two individuals she was now in charge of taking care of.

Sheila didn't protest when Pam told her that she was going to go to Florida with Shirley. She knew that she had been through enough trauma with her kidnapping and the loss of her sister. She also needed to focus on Todd and see if they could fix their strained relationship.

After Jeryca's funeral and after Pam left, Sheila walked into her daughter's old room and looked around. She felt like there was a real emptiness in her home. Her oldest was dead, and as that thought entered her head and her heart she broke down.

Todd came up behind her. "What the fuck are you crying for? You knew that the life your child was living could've ended like this. Man, go fix me something to eat."

Shelia stood up and instantly went into attack mode. Anything she could get her hands on she hit him with. She screamed for him to get the hell out of her house and to never return. She could tolerate almost anything, but her child was dead, and all he could say was that she'd asked for it!

As soon as Todd was out of the house, Shelia called her brother to see if she could stay with him and his wife for a few days.

Sergio and Ramon weren't happy to hear that Jeryca and Orlando had been killed. The fact of the matter was that they still owed them money. They knew that the money didn't just disappear and they wanted it. They called a meeting with Valerie, Desiree, Big Rob, and Alex. They explained that they wanted them to go to Orlando and Jeryca's house and find their money. They didn't care who or what got in their way. They knew that the house was being occupied by Jeryca's baby sister and two other individuals, but they didn't care. They wanted their money, period.

Valerie and Desiree were placed in charge. They were to get in and out without bringing a lot of unnecessary attention to the condo by being noisy and reckless. Once they left Sergio and Ramon, Valerie told Desiree that they would meet later to put their plans in motion.

She had to go to the doctor. Valerie had found out a few weeks earlier that she was three months pregnant by Zack, but she hadn't told anyone. She was still grieving the loss of her man and her friend. She had to figure out a way, and quickly, to keep Jeryca's little sister from getting hurt. She was tired of all the killings. She was tired of being in the game, period. She wanted out, but she knew death would be her only option if she didn't do something fast. She couldn't move sloppily, though.

She had plenty of money saved and could make it on half of it. She had to find someone she could trust to help her, but who? She wasn't going to be responsible for any innocent child losing their life for something they had nothing to do with. Valerie drove around for a while and figured the only person she could call on was the woman who had taken care of Pam and Jeryca their entire lives: Shelia. She knew she had a man who was as greedy as Sergio and Ramon, and she hoped that Shelia had enough love and respect for her kids to want to help. It was going to take a lot of planning, but she could make it work if she planned carefully.

Two Days Later

Shelia arrived in Virginia early in the a.m. She was greeted at the train station by her brother,

Barry, and her sister, Angela, whom she hadn't seen in years. They had lost touch over the years, but Shelia had no one else she could turn to. Her sister embraced her long and tight. Sheila, finally feeling the strain, crumbled to the floor and began to cry. Her brother raced over and grabbed her as she hit the floor. They carried her out of the train station and put her in the car.

For the first few days, she slept constantly. It was the only way to escape the reality of her child being dead. She realized that everything that her kids had been through was because of her. She wasn't eating and her brother's wife, Tasha, was very worried about the woman she had just met. She didn't know much about her, but she knew that her sister-in-law was deep in mourning.

"Baby, don't you think you need to get your sister up? She hasn't really eaten since she has been here. Let's try to get her up and out for a while," Tasha said.

Barry looked at his wife and sighed. "You're right. I just don't know what to say to her. Angela has been calling and asking about her as well. Maybe I need to call her and see if she would like to take her out together. With both of us there she may come to life a little."

"Yes, because she can grieve herself to death if y'all don't do something," Tasha replied.

Tasha went to check on Sheila while Barry called Angela. They decided to take Sheila out the following day.

Sheila agreed to go out to dinner with her brother and sister the following day as long as they let her rest that night.

Sheila was out with her brother and sister when her phone rang. She first thought it was Pam calling but upon answering it, she learned it wasn't. After hearing everything that the caller said, she looked at her brother and shook her head. "How in the hell did I let things get this way with my family? I've been such a bad mother. What can I do?"

"Baby girl, what's wrong?" her brother asked.

"That was an old friend of Jeryca's. Her name is Valerie, and she just informed me that some men are planning on killing Pam because Jeryca owed them money. I can't lose another child," Sheila cried.

"What else did she say?" Angela asked.

Sheila filled them in on everything and told her brother that she didn't have anyone she could send to help her daughter. Barry looked at his two sisters and dropped his head. He couldn't let Pam die knowing he could've helped.

He told Sheila to call back and let him talk to Jeryca's friend so he could get an idea of what was going to happen. Sheila called Valerie back, and after Barry heard all the details, he agreed to go. He told his two sisters not to mention anything to Tasha because she would flip out and he didn't want that. Instead, they were going to tell her that he was going down to Florida to see if he could convince Pam to come back and see her mother. He was going to tell Tasha that Pam would probably listen to him since they used to be close.

Over the next three days, Barry and Sheila talked to Valerie on a regular basis, and it was decided that Sheila was in no shape to help them, even though she fought to go. Barry was to leave on Wednesday morning on the bus to Florida. Valerie was going to have a friend of hers pick him up. She told him that if everything went okay, he would be leaving Florida with a bountiful amount of cash. She told him to expect to be gone for at least two weeks but no more than four. They had to execute her plan with care because any slip could get all of them killed, including Pam.

Three weeks after Sergio and Ramon instructed Valerie and Desiree to find the money that Orlando and Jeryca owed him, Valerie was ready to make her move. She called Sergio and asked if he had seen Desiree. She told him that she needed to see when she would be ready to check Orlando and Jeryca's condo. Desiree and two of Sergio's men had staked out the condo, but while they were staking out the condo, Barry and Terry were staking them out. Valerie made sure they that they knew everything they needed to know. Terry was an old player who used to run drugs for Ramon, but Ramon caught him using the drugs instead of selling them. Terry went into hiding but kept in touch with Valerie from time to time. Valerie knew he would be willing to help her take out Sergio and Ramon just so he could come out of hiding.

After Valerie learned Desiree's whereabouts, she called her sister Hanna and told her and Jeff to meet her at Westfield Estates where Desiree lived. She knew she would be there alone because Ramon and Sergio were at the office.

After forty minutes of driving, Valerie pulled up and instructed Hanna and Jeff to wait for her to text them before they pulled up. She had two hours to do everything she had to do before Sergio came home.

She pulled up to the gate and pushed the button. Desiree answered, "Who is it?"

"It's me, girl! Open the dang gate." Valerie laughed.

"Oh, shut up! Give me a second."

As the gate opened, Valerie double-checked her purse to make sure the syringe filled with Ativan was in close range. Valerie had no intention of killing Desiree. She just needed her out of the picture for a few days in order for her plan to go smoothly. Valerie got out the car and Desiree met her at the door.

"Bring yo' ass on up in here, bitch."

"I'm coming, slut! What's up with you, bae?" Valerie asked as she walked up on the porch.

"Shit, just waiting on your slow ass to come in the house. Shit, you know a bitch don't do heat." Desiree laughed.

"I'm here now. I was just coming through to make our arrangements for this shakedown," Valerie told her.

"Well, come on in the kitchen. I'm cooking dinner." Desiree headed toward the kitchen with Valerie following close behind.

"So how do you think we can do this without hurting innocent children?" Valerie asked.

Desiree turned and looked at Valerie with a frown. "Shit, I don't want to hurt anybody but you know the code we live by: spare no one and leave no witnesses. Hell, when did you start caring about the kids?" Desiree asked, turning to take her roast out the oven. When she bent down, Valerie quickly walked over, stuck the needle in Desiree's shoulder, and pulled her back up against her to push every single drop into Desiree's body.

Before she pulled it out, she whispered to Desiree, "I started caring when I found out I was having a kid!" When she pulled the needle out, she moved back fast knowing Desiree was going to swing away.

Desiree swung, screaming, "Bitch, what did you do to me?"

"I didn't kill you. That's all that's important!" Valerie answered as she danced around to avoid being hit.

After a few minutes, Desiree started getting dizzy and seeing double. Her movement slowed, and she was very confused. She staggered as she walked and then her body slowly began to fall to the floor. Valerie knew that the fall would probably leave Desiree bruised, but she couldn't catch her. She didn't want to risk hurting herself or her baby.

She called Jeff and Hanna and told them to drive on down. She opened the gate, and all three got to work. After they finished, they dragged Desiree's limp body to the van they'd parked in the garage, tied her up, and put duct tape on her mouth. The three pulled off and headed to the hotel to meet Barry and Terry. They had to play their cards just right to get the money and Sergio and Ramon, killing two birds with one stone.

"Ramon, have you heard from Big Rob or Alex? They should've been back with our money!" Sergio asked.

"No, and I tried to call Alex a few times. That's why we should've sent Valerie and Desiree to get our shit! Let's go see if we can locate their asses. Call Credo and tell him to get Jay and the rest of the crew and meet us at the house ASAP! We took a loss fucking with Orlando and Zack. I ain't taking no more!" Ramon replied.

As they closed up the office and jumped in their black Benz, Sergio dialed Credo's number and told him to meet them at the house. Credo knew that if he and Jay were being called out, it meant murder!

Pam and Travis were outside in front of the condo, playing with the football. A few of the neighbors' children joined them, which made Travis very happy. Pam pretended to be happy for Travis's sake, but she missed her sister something awful. She slept in her sister's room and wore a lot of her clothes. Pam hadn't been enrolled at school because they needed Sheila to sign guardianship papers over to Shirley. They had been calling her repeatedly but to no avail. Pam prayed that her mother was all right. Even though she was very much put off by her mother, she still loved her and didn't want to see her hurt.

As each day passed, Pam was feeling more and more of the empty void that was left in her heart the day Jeryca was taken from her. She had no one to talk to, no one to vent to, and no one to really make her feel better. Being with Shirley and Travis was cool and all, but she needed her sister. Jeryca was her rock and motivator. All she had left of her sister were a few clothes, pictures, and the letter: the last words left for her from her big sis.

Pam had to fake being somewhat happy to keep Travis afloat. He had grown attached to her in the short amount of time that she had been there. Everywhere she went he was right there, which she didn't mind.

She forced herself to smile, laugh, and play. Shirley attempted to talk to her about Jeryca, but Pam brushed it off. Shirley was a sweet woman, but Pam craved her mother's attention. It just really hurt Pam that her mother chose a man over her and her sister. Even so, Pam wanted her around. She felt like, at a time of grief, she needed that family love.

Pam smiled as Travis ran over to her, jumping up and down. "Did you see, Pammy? I threw the ball far!"

"Oh, yes, I saw, and that was very good, Travis. Let's see you do it once more. Throw it to that young man over there," Pam said, pointing to one of the little boys who had asked to play with Travis.

Shirley stood at the door gazing out at the kids. She hadn't seen Travis that happy in a long time, and she was grateful that Pam was there to make it happen. Although Pam was troubled and filled with her own sadness, she always thought of Travis first. She admired that.

"Are y'all ready to eat?" she asked them.

"Yeah!" Travis yelled. He told his new friends good-bye and ran inside.

"Hey, go wash your hands before you go in that kitchen, boy," Shirley yelled.

"Okay, Grandma."

Pam walked in and sat down on the couch. Shirley stood in the doorway watching her. "Come on, Pam, you got to eat a little something too."

"I'm not really hungry right now. I will eat a little bit later," Pam said in almost a low whisper.

"You said that yesterday, and you didn't eat. So no, ma'am, come on now and eat with us," Shirley demanded in a soft voice.

Pam smiled and went and washed up and sat down with them. They grasped hands as Shirley blessed the food. "All right, dig in," Shirley said.

Shirley had worked hard preparing the food she cooked, and everything smelled delicious. She had fixed a roast smothered in gravy, onions and carrots, collard greens, yams, and cornbread.

Pam fixed herself a small plate and ate as she watched Shirley cut up Travis's food. She watched as he devoured it. She loved the way the two connected, but that also made her sadder.

After she ate, she went into her room, locked her door, and cried until she fell asleep. She dreamed of Jeryca every night, which eased her spirit some. She felt like it was Jeryca's way of letting her know she was at peace.

Pam woke up early the next morning and went for a walk around the neighborhood. It was the first time she had ventured out alone since being there. She was still cautious since being kidnapped and learning about everything that her sister had been involved in, but she decided she couldn't live in a box the rest of her life. She walked past a gray Chevy and noticed two guys sitting in it. She sped up and walked to an open area where there were a few people standing around.

"You got to chill, girl!" she murmured to herself.

She looked around and noticed for the first time how beautiful the neighborhood truly was. She wondered if Jeryca had ever taken the time to just look upon the beauty of the community. She sighed and continued walking.

Thirty minutes later she was back home and had a genuine smile on her face. She had actually ventured out by herself and released her fear of being alone outside. She was proud. What would seem simple to others was a big milestone for her.

Chapter Twenty-one

Barry called Sheila to let her know how things were going. "Yeah, I think I should be home soon. But listen, while we were outside the condo I think I got a glimpse of Pam. She looked just like the picture you showed me. Lord, if she isn't a mini you!" He laughed.

"How did she look? What was she doing? Did she look happy?" Sheila threw out question after question.

"Yeah, she looked fine, but I wouldn't say happy. After all of this is over with, I think you need to reach out to her, Sheila. You two are all you have. Well, outside of me and Angela, that is."

"She don't want to see me. I've done way too much." Sheila sighed.

"That's your child. It's never too late, sis. But listen, I got to go. I will call you later. I love you, and tell my wife I love her and will see her soon," Barry said before hanging up. Barry placed his phone in his pocket and joined Valerie and the rest of the team in the sitting area.

"Okay, y'all," said Valerie, "my guys have just informed me that they got Sergio's two delivery guys hemmed up. They were successful in getting the money and by now, if I know my bosses like I think I do, they should be heading home. Has anyone checked on Desiree? I don't want any harm to befall her. She is my best friend, and I love her. So remember that."

Valerie had one person watching Sergio's house for her, and they were to let her know when they arrived home. About twenty minutes passed, and finally, her cell phone rang. She smiled as she showed everyone the video feed of Ramon, Sergio, and their crew entering the house.

Inside the house, Ramon immediately called out to Desiree. After getting no answer, he searched the home. It was odd to him to find her car in the garage but the house empty. He called her cell phone and frowned as he heard it ringing inside the drawer in their bedroom.

"Ay, Sergio, something isn't right, man. Desiree isn't anywhere to be found."

"And why is that weird?" Sergio asked.

"Her car is still in the garage!" Ramon yelled.

"She probably left with someone."

"Well, she wouldn't have left without her phone or her gun!" Ramon said, holding both items up.

"That's true. What the hell is going on?" Sergio frowned, scratching his chin. He called out for the guys to go out and search the grounds for Desiree, but when Credo opened the front door there was a loud click then a huge boom! The house started blowing up section by section, killing everyone inside.

Valerie got the confirmation she needed as she was sent a live feed of Ramon and Sergio's house ablaze. Everyone cheered and congratulated each other on a job well done.

Valerie raised her hand to get everyone's attention. "Well done, fellas, but our job ain't done yet. Let's go get this money!"

Valerie had grabbed Desiree's keys from the table when they kidnapped her so that they could access the office once Ramon and Sergio were dead. She called her two buddies and told them to bring Ramon and Sergio's runners to their office immediately. Hearing that, Valerie's goons knew that everything was a success. They did as they were told and once everyone was in place, they ransacked the entire office. They found the two safes that Valerie knew about and opened them up to find money and jewelry inside. Valerie and Desiree had been with the guys for so long that they were trusted and privy to all the guys' information.

Valerie felt good knowing that she had saved two children's lives. She just wouldn't have been able to live with that weighing on her spirit. She knew that if Ramon and Sergio didn't care about those two kids' lives, they sure wouldn't care about taking her child's life if they had to.

Desiree was awake and allowed to watch television. They kept the channel on the news station. A news bulletin alert flashed on the screen: Uncontrollable fire raged out of control finally contained. Fire crews find several bodies inside, which have not been identified. Stay tuned as we develop and learn more on this top news special.

Desiree frowned and felt the tears gather up in her eyes as she realized that the house that was destroyed was hers, and there was no doubt in her mind that Valerie was the cause of it. Although she realized that Valerie had saved her life, she also realized that Valerie destroyed her life. Ramon was all she knew and all she had. She would never forgive Valerie for what she had done.

Valerie met with everyone at the hotel once they cleaned the office out, and they split the money down the middle. She was going to take her money and disappear, and she was going to take the only threat to Pam and her family with her. She would have to sedate her to get her on Ramon and Sergio's yacht and then dump her on an island far away from Florida. That would give Barry and Sheila enough time to convince Shirley and Pam that they needed to relocate. She planned to leave Desiree with enough money to start over wherever she wanted to.

Pam sat in her room with a pile of clothes on her bed. She decided that she needed to pack some of Jeryca's clothes up. She had so many memories everywhere and needed to clean up some of them. She rummaged through all of Jeryca's jewelry boxes, and as she looked through the second one, she saw the pendant that she had made Jeryca when she was only in the third grade. She couldn't believe Jeryca had kept it all those years. She held it up and smiled. "I love you too, Jeryca."

A few seconds later she heard the doorbell ring and a flood of voices. She got up and walked to the living room to see what was going on. When she walked in she was surprised to see her mother with three other people. She didn't move, afraid of what was about to take place.

"What are you doing here?" Pam asked.

Sheila cleared her throat nervously. "Well, Pam, I'm not here to cause any problems at all. I just wanted to see you. I brought you something, if you want it."

Pam noticed that her mother's hands were shaking as she held out a small box.

"It's not much. It's something that I wanted you to have," Sheila explained.

Pam didn't move, not because she didn't want to, but because she couldn't.

"Please, take it, Pam. Please," she begged.

Pam slowly walked toward her mother and took the box. She never removed her eyes from her mother's.

"It's a pair of earrings that Jeryca had given me. I know it's not much, but I needed to give them to you," she said quietly. Tears were forming in her eyes as she silently prayed that Pam would say something.

Pam opened the box and looked at the earrings. "Thank you. I love them."

"I'm glad. How have you been? Ugh, that's a crazy question. Don't answer that," Sheila said shakily.

"No, I will tell you. I'm not doing great, but I'm gradually getting better. I miss my sister every day but being with Shirley and Travis helps."

Sheila dropped her head, feeling awful that it took someone else to embrace her daughter at this time.

Pam looked up at her mother and finished: "I miss you, though, and I need you so that we can grieve together. It hurts me knowing that I have you out here but can't be with you." Pam started crying uncontrollably. Sheila reached out and grabbed her daughter like she had never done before and hugged her as tight as she could. They stood there for a long period of time crying and consoling one another.

Shirley shook her head wishing she could hold her child once more like that. She hoped that Sheila would do the right thing for once.

Barry cleared his throat to remind Sheila that they were there. Sheila rubbed Pam's hair down and stepped aside a bit. Still holding her child, she smiled and said, "Pam, this is your uncle Barry and aunt Angela. Do you remember them?"

Pam shook her head, and Barry attempted to remind her: "I used to take you fishing when you were yay high." She shook her head again. "Well, no matter. We can get reacquainted if that's okay," he finished.

Pam shook her head yes, and they all sat down. Barry told Shirley and Pam about the recent events that had taken place around them, and Pam and Shirley both remembered hearing about the house that burned down. They told them that they needed to relocate as soon as possible because it wasn't safe for them at that location. Barry explained that there may be other people who believed that Jeryca and Orlando had hidden treasures within their condo.

Sheila reassured Pam that she wouldn't interfere in anything if that's how she wanted it. She just wanted her to be safe. After much consideration, they agreed that they needed to leave Florida.

They would go on to pack up the house with several of Pam's relatives helping. It seemed like a real family atmosphere. Pam didn't want to lose her mother again. She wanted to stay with Shirley and Travis, and she would spend weekends with her mother at Barry's. Pam learned that Sheila was attending church regularly, had gotten a job, and was seeing a psychologist weekly.

***

Three years had passed since the deaths of Ramon and Sergio. Desiree had started a new life in Hawaii. She never returned to Florida because for her there were just too many memories. She couldn't get past the fact that Valerie had betrayed them all for her own selfish needs. She vowed that if they ever crossed paths again, she would kill her on the spot. She did appreciate that Valerie had left her with enough money to start fresh. That was the least the bitch could do, in her mind.

As she walked the beach of Hawaii, she took in the cool, fresh breeze that swept past her. Oh, how she wished that Ramon was there with her. She walked along the shore barefoot and lost in thought, not realizing that she was being watched.

"Dana, come on. Let's walk the beach," Emily shouted.

Dana's legs had made almost a complete recovery, and she was walking. It was still hard for her to maneuver on stairs and it caused her a small amount of discomfort walking on concrete surfaces, but she was now out of the wheelchair and was using a cane to walk. Her burns were still very much visible, but she had learned to

accept them. They were a part of her and day
by day she was embracing them. She still had
trust issues, but after all the awful things she
had done, she would try not to judge others too
harshly.

She had asked Rone if he could check on
Brittany for her, because outside of him and
Emily, Brittany was the only one who loved her
and stayed loyal to her 100 percent. He had
called and learned that because of her mental
stability she hadn't been tried and most likely
wouldn't be. She was still in the mental hospital,
but she wasn't talking to anyone, nor was she
interacting with anyone. It was reported that all
she did was sit in her room or in the day room,
spaced out.

Dana wanted to see her friend badly but was
told it was too early for her to travel back to New
York. Dana was declared legally dead, but Rone
didn't want to chance going back so soon. Emily
volunteered to go pay Brittany a visit and report
to them on her condition. Rone agreed that that
would be a great idea.

As Dana and Emily were walking along the
beach they passed a familiar face, a face Dana
often dreamed about: the bitch who drenched
her with gasoline. Dana paused when she
saw her but said nothing. Emily saw the look

on Dana's face and frowned. She didn't ask any questions at first. They just continued to walk the shore. The woman Dana saw didn't recognize her at all. Hell, she didn't seem like she recognized anything, in Dana's opinion.

"Okay, Dana, who the hell was that lady you were just staring a hole into?" Emily asked as soon as they were far enough away to where Emily could look at her without being noticed.

"That was the bitch who drenched me with gasoline. She was with Jeryca. I don't even know her name, but that's that bitch! I dream about her every other night! She tried to help them kill me!" Dana cried angrily.

"Are you sure, Dana?" Emily asked.

"I'm freaking positive. You remember when I told you about the scar on the woman's chin?" Dana asked.

"Yes, I remember," Emily said after thinking back. "I'll be right back. Don't go anywhere."

Emily walked toward where Desiree was walking and starting running and pretended to fall into her as she approached her. "Oh, I'm so sorry. Please forgive me," Emily said, helping the lady up and taking time to check her face out.

"Bitch, watch where the hell you're going next time," Desiree growled.

Emily refrained from cussing her out. "Again, my apologies." Emily ran off and headed toward Dana but made sure to not run directly for her. She turned back around and saw that Desiree was out of sight and she walked over to Dana.

"Well?" Dana said.

"Not her. The lady doesn't have any scars at all," Emily replied. "Come on, let's go back home and relax. I'm tired."

"But I could've sworn—" Dana started but was interrupted.

"Dana, darling, it wasn't her," Emily said.

Emily and Dana returned to their beachfront home and relaxed for the remainder of the day.

The next morning Dana got up and took a bath. She got dressed and went to the kitchen looking for Emily. She was nowhere to be found, but an hour later Emily walked in sweating and breathing heavy.

"Where you been? You had me worried sick!" Dana fussed.

"I went for a jog, Mother!" Emily laughed. "I'ma take a shower right quick and make you breakfast."

"I had cereal already," Dana said, but when she turned Emily had already disappeared into the bathroom.

When Emily emerged, she told Dana that she had to leave in an hour to catch a plane back to New York. She asked Dana if she needed anything done before she left. She was going to be gone for a week and would return hopefully with some good news about Brittany. Dana told her that she would be okay until Rone returned, and to call her as soon as she landed.

After Emily left, Dana went out on the balcony to get some fresh air, and she saw several police trucks on the beach. She called Rone to see if he was okay, and when he answered, she sighed a breath of relief. "Good, you're okay."

"Yes. Why you say that?" he asked.

"I just saw a bunch of police out on the beach and was just checking on you," she replied.

"Yeah, I'm good. I should be back in a little while, dear."

"Take your time, Rone. Tell your friend I said hello and can't wait to meet her."

"Will do, my darling daughter," he said.

She hung up and went back to the balcony to be nosy. She was just recently getting used to him calling her his daughter. Life was definitely surprising to her. Dana decided to go and take a nap while it was quiet.

She awoke a while later and went and sat down and turned the television on. As soon as she sat down, she again saw the face that she had dreamed about, flashing on the screen. "Desiree

Fontana's body washed up on the Hawaiian shore. Police are looking for anyone who may be related to her and can positively identify the body. If you have any information, please contact Hawaii police. In other news . . ."

"I knew it was her!" Dana shouted. The scar was very much still visible, but why did Emily say it wasn't her? Why had Emily lied? Dana's mind started clicking. Emily wasn't here when she got up, nor had Rone come in that night. He had found a lady to spend time with, but he never stayed out all night. Matter of fact, he was there when she went to bed last night. When did he leave? And why was Emily leaving for New York all of a sudden?

Dana's mind started formulating its own theory of what happened. She smiled inside but was upset that she wasn't included in anything.

Emily called later on. "Hey, I made it to New York safely. I'm going to check into my hotel and relax, and will be going to see Brittany."

"I'm glad you made it safely, but I have a bone to pick with you," Dana exclaimed.

"What kind of bone?" Emily asked curiously.

"You know what I'm talking about!" Dana groaned. "What did you do this morning?"

"Dana, I have no idea what you're talking about. But I'm about to go. I love you, cousin," Emily said.

Dana laughed. "I love you too, cousin."

After they hung up, Dana realized it didn't matter what they had done. She knew they did it out of love. That still didn't change that she had questions.

She sat back on the couch and waited for Rone to come in. She was going to see if she could pry some information from him. How could he resist his daughter? Dana laughed out loud as the thought crossed her mind.

Chapter Twenty-two

Emily woke up bright and early the following morning, got dressed, and headed out the door to go to the mental hospital to visit Brittany. As she walked the familiar streets, she realized that she missed New York. It was home! She took pictures to show Dana all the wonderful changes that she was seeing.

As she approached the institute, she took out her ID and entered. She was patted down and escorted to the visiting room. She sat for a few minutes then finally she met Brittany's eyes. Even though Brittany dropped her head, Emily knew that Brittany recognized her.

Once she was seated, Emily reached out for her hands, but Brittany pulled back and placed her hands in her lap, still looking down. Emily looked around and started talking. "Brittany, I know you know who I am, but I need to see your face, sweetie. Look at me please."

Brittany looked up, and tears filled her eyes instantly.

"Oh no, baby girl, ain't no freaking crying! Wipe those tears away!" Emily said.

Brittany did as Emily said, and Emily smiled. "That's right. Listen, I got some news for you: you are going to leave this muthafucka this week. Rone has been working on something that has worked once before, and it's gonna work this time. Do you hear me? You ain't got to do anything but look at me to let me know you understand what I'm saying."

A few seconds passed, but Brittany looked up once again.

Emily started whispering, "All right now, listen: there will be a new guard placed by your room for the next two nights. Don't be alarmed, 'cause he will be one of Rone's guys. That's all I'ma say right now. Just don't be afraid or get aggressive, no matter what! Okay? Look at me again to let me know you understand me."

Brittany once again looked up, but said nothing and then dropped her head again. Emily shook her head in sadness at Brittany's appearance. Her hair was matted, her clothes were dingy, and her face looked old. She was gray and distant.

"I will see you soon, okay?" Emily sighed. She wanted to cry at the way Dana's dear friend looked, but she couldn't break. Not when they were so close to getting her out. Emily had to make sure that Rone's friend was going to be at the dock waiting for them, and she had to make last-minute arrangements. Dana would be so happy when she returned.

She left the hospital and grabbed a taxi and got dropped off at the dock. She met with three guys Rone had sent to meet her. They worked diligently to prepare for Friday.

When Friday approached, Emily was getting nervous. She waited at the pier, and the guys were running late. She prayed that they didn't get caught up. As she paced back and forth, Rone called.

"Hey, are y'all en route?"

"They haven't even gotten here yet!" Emily replied.

"What! Let me call and see what the holdup is. They better not double-cross me 'cause I can still get their asses hemmed up!"

Rone hung up. Now Emily was even more concerned. She hoped they weren't going to trap her and have her arrested.

As she continued to pace she saw headlights approaching. She ran and hid behind the small building that sat on the pier. She watched as two men pulled a stretcher from the back of an ambulance. She walked slowly around the building and walked over to the men. "Is that her?"

"Yeah. We had a little problem getting her to eat her food, so we had to switch up and put it in with her medication. She will probably be out for the entire trip. Tell Rone we are even!" the driver said.

"All right, I will do that. Thank you, though, for helping and keeping it real with us," she said.

"It's cool. Y'all better get going. Daylight will be peeping around soon," he said.

Emily thanked them again and got on the yacht and they peeled out. She checked on Brittany to make sure she was okay. She looked so peaceful, like she was really dead. Emily shook the thought out of her head. She sat back to enjoy the rest of the ride, which would take them down the coast a little to a plane home.

Brittany hadn't said a word to Emily the whole trip, but she looked almost calm. At the Kona airport, Emily hailed a cab. They both got in and sat back. The driver looked back at them and asked for their destination. Emily gave them the address and looked over at Brittany. "Are you good, ma?"

Brittany nodded, but Emily could see sadness in her eyes. Hopefully, that was about to change. They road in silence, and once they arrived at their house, Emily helped her get out of the car. Dana had no idea what was going on, nor did she know that Emily was returning that day.

Once they walked up the walkway, Emily told Brittany to knock on the door while she carried in their belongings. Brittany knocked on the door and waited. She knocked again, but still there was no answer. She looked at Emily, confused, until the door opened and Rone motioned for her to come in.

"Hey, Ms. Lady. Come on in and take a load off."

Brittany smiled. It was good seeing a familiar face for once. She knew Emily, but she knew Rone a little better.

"Who is it at the door?" Dana yelled.

"Come and see for yourself," Rone yelled back.

Brittany sat up and looked in the direction that the voice came from, frowning and looking from Emily to Rone. Yet again, she had tears gathering up in her eyes.

Dana walked out and stopped in her tracks as she glared at Brittany. "Hell no! No!" she cried. "Tell me y'all aren't playing with me!" She walked slowly over to Brittany who, at this point, was also shocked. "Britt, is it really you?"

Brittany looked confused, but for the first time in years, she spoke slowly. Her words were almost inaudible, but she spoke. "Yes. Oh, my God! Is it you?"

"How? I mean, who . . ." Dana was tongue-tied. She hugged Brittany tight, and Brittany hugged her back. She was in total shock, but it was the greatest feeling she had had in a long time.

The two hugged for what seemed like hours until Rone separated them. "All right, you two, let's sit down and talk."

Brittany and Dana sat side by side, and they talked for hours. Rone told Brittany that he got Dana out the same way he got her out. He couldn't leave her in there, let alone keep her thinking that Dana was dead, not after everything she had sacrificed.

Brittany and Dana decided to walk the beach that night with Emily. It was the Three Musketeers forever! Dana felt great again, and despite all the hurtful events in her life of late, she knew that she had found true friends. Indeed, they were the very definition of Queen Hustlaz.